Crescent Ridge Mail Order Brides Books 1-4

Jacqueline Carmine

Contents

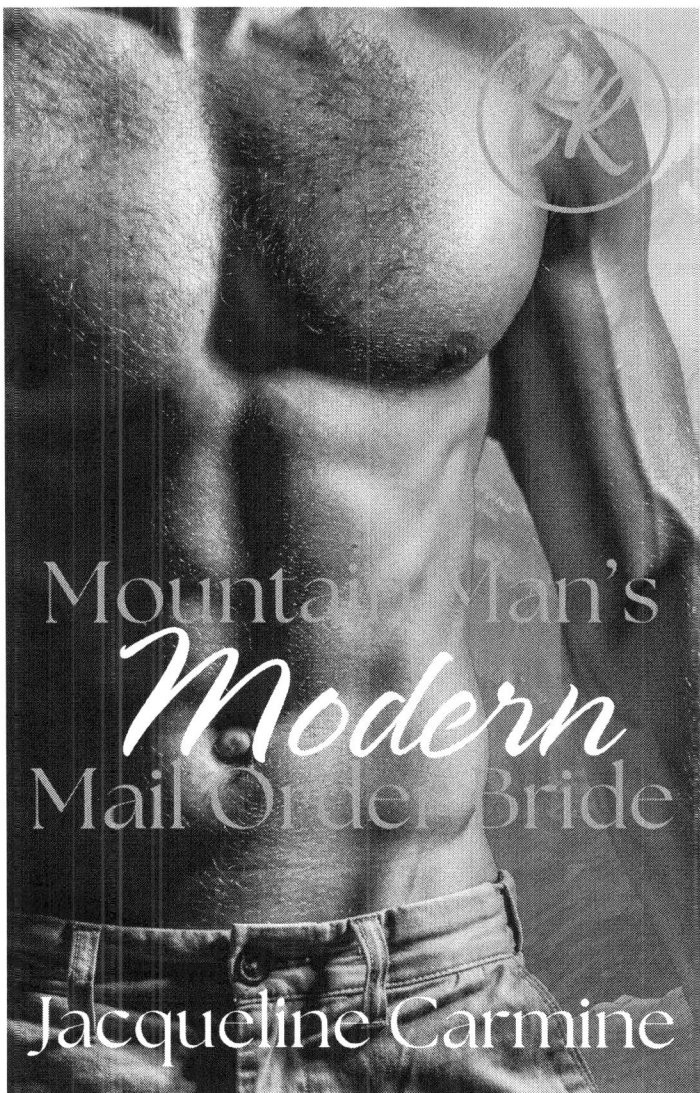

Mountain Man's *Modern* Mail Order Bride

Jacqueline Carmine

Contents

June 17

Ms. Porter,

I received your profile from Pearl's Matchmaking. Looking it over, we don't have much in common, in fact I would worry that Pearl is setting her business up for failure, but our dealbreakers match exactly. I believe love can grow from respect and companionship but dealbreakers don't change.

To be blunt, I want marriage and a large family. I'm an only child and since my father's death left myself and my mother on our own to take care of each other I want my children to have a larger family to lean on.

It's hard to find a partner when my hometown is so small, and I don't get many opportunities to venture out. My mother has been encouraging me to leave Crescent Ridge for years to find a wife. But she's getting older, and I don't like being too far away from her in case she needs me.

If you would be amenable, I would like to discuss your long-term goals and plans for the future.

Respectfully,

Daniel Hart

June 24

Daniel,

I wasn't expecting to receive a letter, but I love the nostalgic touch. It's been so long since I've written a letter. I'm afraid my handwriting is a mess. Please don't judge me.

I've been career driven for as long as I can remember. I write romance novels. That's not included in my profile. Not much is included if I'm honest. It's difficult to put my dreams onto paper to be shared with strangers. But I suppose you're no longer a stranger and if you can be so open and blunt then so can I. I want to be a wife and have at least three children. I want my husband to be respectful, faithful, and kind. I want to continue writing. My books sell reasonably well, and I enjoy writing them. I have a dog named River who is a chocolate lab mix that I adopted from the local shelter. I decided to get a dog after my last break up, two years ago. I didn't want to waste any more time dating men who weren't serious about committing to me.

I don't expect a fairytale, but I can't settle for anything less than exactly what I want.

Sincerely,

Lily

July 1

Lily,

You'll find no judgement here. The letters are because while the town has Wi-Fi my cabin doesn't and cell reception on the mountain is spotty at best.

I want five children, but I could settle at three. If you can write your books in the most remote section of the Viridian Mountains, I see no reason for you to stop doing what you love.

I spend my days running around the ridge from one job to the next. Crescent Ridge doesn't have a plumber, an electrician, or even a contractor. People like to hire locally, and no one from the city wants to make the drive up to the ridge to fix someone's leaky faucet.

Respect, fidelity, and kindness set the bar low Lily. I can promise those and add that if you marry me, you will have my protection, support, and loyalty. You'll never have to settle again as long as I live. This I can promise with confidence.

Yours,

Daniel

July 3

Ms. Porter,

At Mr. Hart's request I've attached a marriage license to this email. In the span of three weeks, you and Mr. Hart have broken my record for fastest courtship. Something must be said for the romance of letter writing in this digital age. I wish you and your fiancé all the best. Congratulations on your upcoming marriage.

Warm wishes,

Mrs. Pearl Winslow

Daniel

Crescent Ridge, CO

If my mother knew what I did she would smack the back of my head. She wouldn't judge me for using a matchmaker. The population on the ridge is tiny. The only single women are a group of recent graduates too young for a thirty-two-year-old man and a few of my mother's friends who are widowed or divorced.

No, she wouldn't be upset about the matchmaking. She would be mad as hell at how I proposed marriage to Lily. Contacting the service to send her a marriage application was jumping the gun. Hell, I didn't even ask her to marry me. No woman is going to marry a guy who promises the bare minimum after two letters.

I sent the request off to Pearl at the end of a long day running around the ridge from one cabin to the next. The

Kincaid's needed their roof patched, and Jon can't climb a ladder until his foot finishes healing. Flora Williams needed a load of firewood dropped off. She likes to be prepared in case the winter storms start rolling in early. On her next birthday she'll be sixty but that doesn't bother her much. She can keep her cabin maintained but she can't chop and haul the firewood with her bad hip.

It was a long day and when I walked into my cold cabin after sundown with all the lights off, I felt a keen loneliness that I couldn't shake. The next day I drove down to town and fired off a quick email to Pearl. An hour later I was cursing technology and my own foolishness. I couldn't take the email back and I've felt unsteady on my feet ever since.

I've really screwed up this time. Over the past weekend I've been trying to write Lily another letter explaining why I'm in such a rush to get married. Explain that like her I've refused to settle for less than I want. I don't like playing games and I just want my wife to come home to at the end of the day. Someone to talk to about my day and someone who can make the cabin I've lived in for the last decade feel like a home.

Someone to help me build a family.

Ever since Pearl sent me Lily's profile I was hooked. One look at her picture with her warm smile dimpling her round cheeks and her big blue eyes shining with laughter behind her large oval glasses and I was obsessed. Suddenly

I could see her waiting for me at the end of a long day. It was her I wanted to tell about my day. No one else would do. I knew it in my soul. In my bones.

I tried to play it cool. Tried to make it seem logical. I couldn't tell her that when I wrote about children, I was picturing girls with her bright eyes and sons with her blonde hair and freckles.

It took me a full week to write a letter that I can only hope conveys my regret at rushing her. I even include my phone number and email. Something I should have given her before attempting to marry her. I might not be able to check either on the mountain, but I can drive down to town daily to check for messages and voicemails. Hell, we've never talked on the phone even. She doesn't know what my voice sounds like.

I park down by the coffee shop *Bean There* before making my way to the post office to drop off the letter. I'm walking down the sidewalk on main street when I hear shouting on the opposite side of the street. Glancing across I see my mother waving her arm and stretching onto her tiptoes to get my attention.

At her side is a curvy and petite blonde with long curly hair facing away from me. She looks familiar but I can't place where I know her from. Maybe she's one of the tourists who married into the Johnson family. She's wearing a blue sundress with a sunflower print with tiny straps holding it in place on her shoulders.

As her companion turns to face my direction my stomach twists into a knot and my mouth goes dry.

Lily.

Lily

Daniel is larger than life. Even from across the street I can tell he's one of the tallest men I've ever met. I have his picture thanks to the matchmaking service but it's just a headshot. There's no concept of scale.

Watching him jog across the street I can't look away. His brown hair is curling above his ears and his sideburns blend into his darker beard that covers his jaw and chin. He wears a red flannel buttoned over a white shirt obviously prepared for the chilly morning in the mountains. I curse my choice of dress for the fiftieth time as a breeze blows through the thin skirt of my dress. Goosebumps run up my arms and I can't tell if it's from the chill or the tight denim jeans covering Daniel's massive thighs.

"So how do you know Daniel?" Mary asks me.

Shaken from my hyper fixation I smile at the older woman. With her short silver hair, she looks like someone's grandmother. Something that was only reinforced when she hugged me after introducing herself.

"I'm his wife," I say just as Daniel reaches us.

Mary's eyes dart to the large man and she raises her eyebrow as her lips pinch together in a frown. Unease turned my stomach leaving me feeling queasy. Twenty minutes in Crescent Ridge and I was already making a terrible impression judging by her look. Daniel glanced at the older woman and winced at her stern look.

"How lovely," she tells him before turning to me with a bright smile. "You'll have to come over for dinner this Friday."

She doesn't wait for my response before she waves goodbye and leaves me standing on the sidewalk with my new husband. Well at least she didn't condemn our marriage outright. Maybe I could win her over with time.

"Hi," I say suddenly shy.

"Hello Lily." His low baritone rumble has my panties damp and my cheeks burning white hot.

"You seem surprised," I tell him as I see the envelope crushed tight in his massive fist.

My eyes widen as I realize why he's surprised. It's a break-up letter. He made a mistake, or the agency did but it doesn't matter. I packed up my apartment and drove cross country to marry a man who doesn't want me.

Tears flood my eyes as I spin away from Daniel. I can bear the embarrassment, but I will not let him see me cry. Our letter exchange hadn't been romantic, but I had felt a connection. I thought we had the foundation to build a legacy. I thought I could fall in love with a man like him.

I want to run away but I'm an adult. Just as I'm about to turn around and listen to his break-up speech Daniel steps in front of me. His brown eyes are still wide, but his mouth is stretched into a grin.

His grin falls as he notices my tears.

"I know I can appear threatening, but I promise you're safe with me Lily. Please don't be scared," he whispers into the cold air between us.

"I'm not afraid of you."

"Then why are you crying?" he asks gesturing to my face.

"You don't want me," I reply waving my hand at the crumpled letter. "You weren't expecting me even though I filled out the form and wrote you about ending my lease."

"I haven't gotten your letter yet," he tells me before stuffing the envelope into his back pocket. "You signed the marriage license?"

"Yes," I reply squeezing my hands into fists at my sides.

I signed that license like a fool. I replied immediately to his letter agreeing to be his wife and forfeited my deposit to end my lease early. Suddenly he swoops down to wrap his arms around my waist, and I'm crushed against his hard chest as he lifts me off my feet and spins us in a fast circle.

"My wife."

"Well not technically. If you didn't know I filled out the application, then you haven't filed it yet."

"That's a quick fix," he says setting me on solid ground and grabbing my hand before leading me down the street.

"You want to marry me?"

"Yes, more than anything."

"Are you sure?"

"Maybe you should read this before we go to the courthouse," he says stopping our progress and handing me the envelope from his back pocket.

July 10

Lily,

Please forgive me. The matchmaking agency has sent me hundreds of dating profiles over the last several months but when I saw your picture, I knew you were the one for me. I haven't reached out to any other matches. I knew if my perfect woman were out there, I would know her on sight. Like you I don't have patience for games or wasting time on frivolous relationships. For me it was such a deep feeling of knowing. I recognized you in my soul as the missing part of me.

Sounds crazy. I know. My parents married the same day they met. My dad said he knew she was his wife from the second he laid eyes on her. I know it sounds superficial to claim you based on your picture. But I've seen the proof of love at first sight my entire life. My parents were married for almost forty years and would still be going strong if not for the car accident that took my dad from us.

I'm sure it's odd and terrifying to have a man you've never met in person confess his love for you through a letter. I find myself wanting to fly out to LA just to see you, but I know how creepy it would be if I just showed up on your doorstep.

I love you, Lily.

I want to know everything about you. Your likes and dislikes. I want to know your favorite foods so I can make you the perfect dinner when you come to Crescent Ridge. I want to marry you, Lily.

I'll wait as long as you want. You don't know it yet, but I'm already wrapped around your finger. Anything you need or want I will provide.

Marry me, Lily.

Marry me so that I can show you how well I will love you. So that I can make you fall in love with me.

Love,

Daniel

Daniel

I watch her read my letter as we stand in the middle of the sidewalk. I should have taken her to the coffee shop so she could sit somewhere warm. After watching her shiver as a gust of wind whips past us I slip out of my flannel and drape it over her bare shoulders.

It hides her freckles from my gaze, but it also covers her from the wandering eyes of the single men local to the ridge. The town might not have many single women, but mountain men like me are in over abundance. Men who were either raised here or relocated for their career. Mountain rescue does a lot of recruiting in the surrounding towns and cities. Plenty rotate out but several stay for the hometown charm and peace and quiet.

I watch as men walk past and seeing their eyes catch on her slim form causes irritation to rise. They know better than to stare. If they entertain the idea of stopping to talk to us my withering glare sends them on their way before they can pause their stride.

Waiting patiently for her to finish and decide our fate I watch her emotions play out on her expressive face. As she reads her smile slowly comes back giving me hope that I haven't bungled this raw connection between us. I've never doubted our fate only how many missteps I would take before she was convinced, I was the one for her. I knew she was the one. I called her to the mountain, and she came.

As she finishes the letter she starts crying again and my stomach drops. Twice now I've made her cry in the span of a few minutes.

Her hand strikes out grabbing my shirt and twisting it tightly into her fist. I let her pull me forward until we're pressed together.

"Yes." Her voice is a mere whisper in the wind. But it's all I need to hear.

"Let's get to the courthouse so we can get married and then I'll get you home."

"I need to pick up River from Mrs. Morrison before we go home."

"She's always loved dogs. I'm not surprised she volunteered to watch him. She has three of her own," I tell her as I wrap my arms around her back, holding her close.

"She insisted once she found out how long our road trip was." Lily says and I notice the slight shadow underneath her eyes. LA is a multi-day drive away from the Viridian Mountains and being the sole driver would be exhausting.

"You need to rest. We can get married tomorrow," I say already mentally switching gears. Our marriage can wait one more day. Moving her entire life all this way is a massive undertaking and I wish I had checked my email and filed the license so it would be one less thing for her to worry about. A small voice reminds me that I didn't think she would accept my proposal, but I dismiss it.

"We could but we're getting married today so I can sleep in tomorrow," Lily says with a shake of her head.

If not for the delicate blush highlighting her cheeks, I would have dismissed Lily's comment as innocent. I'm not the only one feeling the physical pull between us.

"Right this way then," I say as I take her tiny hand in mine again and begin leading her towards the courthouse. It's a small red brick building where I've come in the past to pay my property taxes and file permits for various projects. No one is going to check that the Kincaid's porch is within regulation size, but I always make sure I do the job right.

The upside to filing the license after Lily arrived is that we can have a small ceremony today. My mother will want to celebrate our union with a reception, but this is just for Lily and me.

Our vows are a blur in front of the magistrate. All I can pay attention to is the blonde-haired beauty wearing my flannel in front of me. But when the judge says I can kiss my bride it all snaps into focus.

Lily's lips are pillow soft underneath mine. Willing and eager in my hold the kiss lingers longer than decent.

When I pulled back her face was bright red, but her eyes showed the truth behind her embarrassment. Her arousal blows her pupils wide, and it takes every bit of my control not to pull her in for another kiss.

We need to get River and we need to get up the mountain. It's been chilly all morning and I can smell rain in the air. I have little doubt we're about to get hit with a raging thunderstorm.

I want my wife safe in my cabin, in my bed and under me before that storm hits. I've been dying to have Lily in my bed since I laid eyes on her. Her dress clings to her soft curves and seeing my flannel dwarf her only riles my protective instincts.

Lily

That kiss burns in my mind long after we've left the courthouse. I never had any doubts that we would have chemistry. I just didn't expect a simple kiss to set my body on fire like it did.

We don't talk much as Daniel accompanies me to Morrison's Hardware. The silence is comfortable and as we walk down the quiet streets, I can hear the leaves rustling against each other as a cold breeze blows through the woods surrounding the town. I hear a woodpecker drilling into a tree in the distance as we enter the hardware store.

"Well, if it isn't my best customer and his wife!" a loud voice booms as soon as the bell chimes above the door. Spinning to face the front counter I see a stocky man who stands almost as tall as my husband. His grey beard is bushy and long, but his hair is shorn short. His cheeks are a bright cherry red.

Before we can return his greeting, Mrs. Morrison leads River out of the backroom.

"There you are deary. I figured you wouldn't be long after Mary stopped by to tell us the good news." I give River some head scratches as he runs up to Daniel and begins sniffing his legs.

"Hello Bert. Ellen," Daniel greets both Morrisons before he turns his attention to the fifty-pound lab mix circling his legs like a shark.

Daniel ducks down to offer the lab a hand to sniff and after he's been inspected and approved by my dog, he pets him. River's tail wags as Daniel switches to ear rubs. He'll be busy for a good minute. River loves ear rubs.

"Thank you so much for watching him." I tell the petite woman as she joins her husband behind the counter.

"He was no trouble," she says with a flick of her hand.

She barely reaches her husband's chest, and she is as slim as he is wide. Her dress is a heavy fabric that brushes the floor with every step she takes with a floral print that matches the flower she has woven into her silver updo.

"Congratulations on your marriage, you two," Mrs. Morrison says with a smile warm enough to thaw a glacier.

"Thank you, Ellen," Daniel says as he stands up. "I figured mom would spill the beans quickly."

It takes me a moment but when I realize what he has implied my mouth drops open in shock and embarrassment.

"No!" I exclaim even as he nods.

"Yep." He looks perfectly at ease with the fact that I introduced myself as his wife to my mother-in-law who clearly didn't know that her son was getting married. Her reaction makes so much more sense now.

"Did she even know that you proposed?" I ask as I watch a sheepish look turn his face bashful.

"No," he says quietly.

The Morrisons don't hold back their laughter. By the time the chuckles and giggles fade they are both wheezing and red in the face.

"Mary told us all about it dear," Ellen says with a smile.

"She's gonna hold this one over your head for a long time Daniel," Bert says.

Daniel tips his head back and groans, but I can't muster any sympathy. He brought this upon himself.

And I'm too busy watching his Adam's apple bob to care if he's in hot water with his mother. I want to lick every inch of him and discover if he tastes the same as he smells. A mix of freshly cut pine and cedar. The sooner we get home the sooner the honeymoon can start.

"Lily you must be so tired after driving all the way here. Ya'll need to start heading home soon." Ellen's gentle reminder spurs us to action and the two of us and River are on our way to my car when we're stopped by another member of the community.

"Daniel!" greets a barrel-chested man wearing tight black T-shirt with 'Crescent Ridge Fire Dept' emblazoned in red across the front.

"Shawn. Good to see you, this is my wife, Lily," Daniel says to the blonde man.

The man doesn't seem surprised by the news.

"Mama Mary already came by the station to tell us all that her new daughter-in-law was spoken for," Shawn replies with a grin before stretching out his hand to shake mine. "It's a pleasure to meet you, Lily. You married a good man."

"Nice to meet you, Shawn." With a nod at both of us and some parting pats for River he leaves but not before letting us know that the entire town will be eager to meet me.

Daniel

I love Crescent Ridge. There is just something about a small town and its community. They pull you in and never let you go. Once you live on the ridge there is nowhere else you'll ever want to be.

Except right now.

I swear I love these people like my own kin. But with all their well-wishing we've been stuck on the sidewalk for over an hour. First it was Shawn who was brief and polite to my new bride. Can't really complain about him. He's been a good friend for a long time. But then it was a steady parade of all the Fire and Rescue men down at the station. Each had also been polite, but their gazes had lingered on Lily's curves for far too long.

Then the Johnsons and the Kincaids stepped forward to wish us well. Sally and Bertha could talk an ear of corn into husking itself if you let them go on long enough.

Finally, once everyone and anyone in town had stopped and said hello, I was able to whisk Lily back to her car and give her directions to where I had parked. When she pulled her economical silver sedan next to my four-wheel drive gas guzzling work truck, I thought again about how different we are. A city girl and a mountain man.

Before I get too bogged down in my thoughts, I remember the way she glowed when talking to my mom. How she was kind and warm with everyone she met today, even though she's traveled such a long way and is dead on her feet.

We can make our marriage work. I know we can. I'll talk to a few folks in town tomorrow about letting an office space for Lily to work in. She said she could write from anywhere, but I don't want her to struggle to reach her editor or publisher. I plan to treat her career the same way I treat my own.

Lily's eyes are droopy despite the midday sun beating down.

"Are you sure you're okay to drive?" I ask her one more time.

I want to insist that we take her luggage and stow it in my truck and leave the car behind for a day. But Lily has a determined set to her shoulders, and I have an inkling of what she's going to say before she opens her mouth.

"Yes. I made it all the way here and I only stopped twice for quick naps. I'll be fine."

She returns to her car and waves at me to lead the way up the mountain. As we head up the winding road that will take us high onto the mountain something burns at the edge of my brain. How long were those naps and how long has it been since she slept?

It's a two-day trip from LA. She should have slept more than she did. She shouldn't be driving with so little sleep. I've seen all kinds of wrecks on this road and as we reach a steep grade that has a drop off on one side, I keep half my focus on the road in front of me and half on my rearview mirror.

I can see her blue eyes locked on the road ahead of her and I relax slightly. I'm still mad that she insisted on driving her car, but she is taking the drive seriously. When we get home, and she has slept I'll tell her more about mountain life. How dangerous it can be and how every risk, no matter how small, can have devastating consequences.

My father was sober, bright eyed and bushy tailed when he went over the edge of Waxing Curve. He didn't survive and he had lived on the ridge his entire life, the same as I have.

As we pull into the driveway and the forest parts to reveal my cabin, I hope she finds herself as at home here as I do. What I have to tell her about mountain life might just send her running back to the city.

Daniel

I have to force myself to let Lily go. There is something that feels so right about holding her in my arms in our home. Her curves fit perfectly against my solid mass. Every inch of her if soft and yielding to the harsh lines of my body. An image of us tangled in the bed flashes across my mind and I have to release my hold before she feels the evidence of my arousal.

As much as I want to explore her sinful curves and lick every inch, she needs sleep.

Taking her hand, I led her through the main floor and upstairs to the master suite. She takes off the second I open the door, twirling into the center of the room. Straight across from the door is a partial wall with a window above it. The large triangular window had to be custom made but it's worth every dollar to see Lily's enjoyment of the space.

"You can see the whole mountain range!" she shouts.

"A good portion at least," I tell her. "I like to watch the storms roll in and when it snows the view is amazing."

"I can't wait to see it." She tells me facing the wide window with her back to me. I can hear the awe in her voice and I'm sure she's imaging what the mountains will look like with a heavy cloud of snow on top. As beautiful as it is deadly it's one of many reasons my family has always lived on the ridge.

As she stands at the window, the storm I've been expecting finally rolls in. Thunder rolls through the valley, the loud roar shaking the earth and heralding the rain's arrival. As rain strikes the window in a heavy downpour lightning occasionally strikes, splitting the sky with bright flashes. The strikes appear similar to a web of tree roots reaching down from the clouds to touch the ground.

"We need to talk. The mountain is a dangerous place to live," I tell her. She needs to understand the dangers of living on the mountain. Even if every precaution is taken there is still a great deal of risk.

"Absolutely." Her calm tone takes me by surprise.

"There are black bears and mountain lions and while they shouldn't come up to the house there is no guarantee. The roads get dangerous at night even without rain or snow and the nearest doctor is a thirty-minute drive away."

Lily is facing me fully now with a serious expression pulling the corners of her mouth down. I may have asked her to stay too soon.

"I bought bear mace and I'm willing to carry a gun." Lily's blue eyes grip mine as she walks up to me until we're standing chest to chest. "I did a bit of research once we started writing to each other. I was curious about how you lived."

Hope swells my chest, but I can't let this go. Not yet.

"You shouldn't have driven today." I reach out and tip up her chin when she tries to avoid my gaze. "Getting behind the wheel when you're exhausted can be just as deadly as drunk driving."

I wait for her blue eyes to lift from my chin and the tears I see forming knock the breath from my chest.

"Don't cry. Please don't cry sweet girl," I murmur as I pull her into a hug.

I can count on a single hand the number of times I've seen my mother cry. Comforting a crying woman isn't a skill I've ever possessed.

"I didn't want to be a burden." Her muffled words drive a hammer into my throat.

"You're my wife," I begin still searching for the right words to express myself. "Never a burden."

"It's been just me and River for so long. I just saw the end goal and I didn't think about the danger until I saw the sheer drop off the side of the road."

"Just let me take care of you. Rely on me. Lean on me. I want to take care of you. Your safety and happiness are my top priority now."

"Okay." Her concession is said with a small, relieved sigh. I could punch the air with joy if I weren't still holding my wife. The fact that we're finally alone and she's still wearing that thin blue sundress hasn't escaped my notice. I held her tightly for another moment before I released her and took a step back.

"Now go get a shower and get into bed." Her needs come before my wants. No matter how badly that want feels like a need.

"Will you join me?" she asks before I turn to leave the room to give her privacy. Her eyes are droopy and the shadows under her eyes are darker than they were this morning. As tempting as it would be to join her under the hot spray, I shake my head. I'm not going to let my eagerness to fuck my wife overshadow her needs.

"I'll be a distraction. You need your rest now."

She must see my determination because she nods her agreement. Her eyes linger on me as I leave the room. I know from her molten gaze burning the shirt off my back that she's just as eager as I am.

Lily

I hadn't pictured a cabin like this when I decided to marry Daniel. I was bound and determined to make the best out of whatever rustic shack he had built. So long as he had electricity for my laptop and indoor plumbing, I was prepared to rough it. I watched and read everything I could about living in remote areas and off the grid just in case.

This cabin belongs in a magazine with its large windows and wraparound porch. It's absolutely gorgeous. It's massive and it's a sight to see. Pine wood boards give it a warm look and the dark green trim around the windows and shutters mirrors the living trees surrounding the large clearing where the home sits.

"I know it's a little different than what you're accustomed to living in a bustling city," Daniel begins as he holds my car door open for me.

"It's so much better," I tell him still looking at my new home.

"I'm glad you think so, but the inside is rather plain," he says with a grimace. "It's clean and everything works as it should but I'm not good at decorating."

"No deer heads?" I ask as he grabs my luggage from the trunk.

River is darting around the cabin sniffing every corner and every two steps he has to sniff the ground again.

"No mounted heads I swear. I never took to hunting," he replies carrying my four suitcases up the porch steps.

"No roommates?" I ask just to cover my bases.

Daniel shakes his head.

"This is just for us and our family."

"It's perfect," I tell him as I join him on the porch.

We enter the home, with River running in behind us and I can tell right away Daniel was telling the truth. There's a lot of open space. The living room has couches and a TV but no coffee table or pictures on the wall. He has a single plaid blanket draped over the back of the couch that looks soft and plush.

As I rub the blanket, which is as soft as it looks, Daniel clears his throat.

"I know it's not much," he says rubbing the back of his head.

"This living room is bigger than my apartment," I tell him bluntly. "I can decorate our home."

"So, you'll stay?" he asks, turning his big brown eyes to mine.

"Of course, I will," I tell him stepping forward to wrap my arms around his waist. His arms come around me in return and my head is pillowed against his chest. We stand pressed tight together for a while. His heartbeat is steady and strong under my cheek.

It's too soon to tell him but I know this man was meant to be mine. Mine to love.

Lily

It's dark when I wake up. I didn't want Daniel to leave but after I've taken a hot shower and crawled into his massive sleigh bed sleep comes quickly. With the soft patter of rain striking the window I'm tempted to stay in bed. If my husband was in bed with me, I know I wouldn't leave until I've gotten a taste of what I've been craving since that kiss. Looking around the room I can appreciate the warm tones of the bedroom. It is sparsely decorated but the furniture is a matching set made of oak in a large room with cream walls.

"Feel better?" Daniel asks from the bathroom doorway.

His hair is visibly damp as he runs a white towel over it. His chest is bare, and he has green plaid pajama bottoms on that hang low enough to showcase his muscles. Where most men go to the gym to build visible muscles, Daniel's is a quiet strength. Rather than ripple his muscles are solid and I can't speak for a moment as I ogle his body.

"You have no idea," I reply as I walk into his outstretched arms. Wrapping my arms around his bulk the always present awkwardness I feel around new people is noticeably absent. There is just something warm and calming about my husband.

My husband.

Daniel ducks his head and when our lips meet, I'm lulled into a languid heat. Our lips slide against each other, and I'm hit with images of lazy mornings spent in bed with him. Cool sheets caressing heated skin as our bodies lock together. Lazy sinful mornings.

"I'm so happy you took a chance on me," he says as we pull apart. My hands run down his chest, the dark hairs tickling my palms.

"I was terrified in the best way." I let out a sigh.

All my anticipation and worry seem so far away now that I'm standing here in front of him. He's real. He's solid. And he's far better than anything I could have imagined. I thought I was missing out on living my life. But in truth I was just waiting for this man.

"Not anymore, right?"

"Never again," I vow.

"Lily Hart. My wife," he murmurs against the sensitive skin of my neck. Pleasant tingles spread out from everywhere his lips brush my skin.

"Daniel's wife," I moan in response as he cups my breasts through the thin fabric of my pajama shirt dragging a lazy thumb across my pebbled nipple.

"Mine," Daniel growls before cupping my ass and lifting me off my feet to settle against his chest. Legs wrapped around his hips I cling like a koala as he carries me back to the bed.

"Yours."

He lays on top of me holding most of his weight on his forearms while his lips take possession of mine. As sweet and slow as our previous kisses, this one is filled with urgency. Heat builds between my thighs, and I feel my panties clinging to my damp folds. For all the harshness of his mouth against mine, Daniel's hands glide smoothly and steadily up my shirt and brush my skin with a delicate barely there touch.

His hands burn a path from my hips to my chest and it only feels right to grind my hips up against his, pushing my hot center against his hard body. On the second swivel of my hips, Daniel adjusts his body so that my core brushes his cock. Hard and insistent I feel the heat from his cock through the thin fabric of my silk shorts and his pants.

A button and the tiniest pull of fabric to the side are all that separate us. When I reach down to pull my shorts and underwear to the side, he grabs my hand roughly and drags it above my head. A second later his weight settles fully on me, and my other hand joins the first.

His eyes are dark with passion, his pupils wide and his breath bellowing out.

"You're not rushing me."

"We can go slow next time," I groan as he grinds his cock against my pussy. "I need you now."

"Our first time as man and wife is not going to be a quickie." His voice rumbles through his chest and my thighs slide together trying to gain some traction, some friction to relieve the ache this man, this bastard is building.

"Hurry up or I'll finish without you." I moan as I find just the right angle to cause the head of his cock to hit my clit. It's nothing close to the full act but it gets the job done when Daniel springs off the bed to pull my shorts and panties off in one go.

"You'll finish on my tongue or my cock you little brat." He says before delving between my thighs and licking my slit.

"O-okay." I moan.

Bruises are going to form from his grip on my thighs and I love it. To carry the mark of this man as a residual reminder of his possession thrills me. His harsh grip holds me tightly against his mouth sealing his lips to my pussy.

I'm a mess as his tongue lashes at me. Electric tingles spread through my body chasing any lingering drowsiness away. Threading my fingers through his hair I scratch his scalp with my nails, and his moan vibrates against my clit.

Attempting to slide back from the ticklish sensation, I'm brought short by Daniel's grip on my thighs. His relentless pursuit only serves to drive me closer to the edge.

"Not enough." I cry as I feel my muscles squeeze on empty air. It's the thrill of flying high and then plummeting back to earth. But it's hollow without his cock stretching my walls.

He kisses me before notching the head of his cock at my entrance. Our lips slide against each other as he pushes in slowly.

"Let me in, Angel." He growls into my ear and with his next thrust he fills me to the hilt.

Overstimulated I clamp down on his cock as another orgasm crests over me. His ragged breathing hits my ear as I come back down from the high.

"I'm not going to last if you keep squeezing me like that Angel." He growls sending vibrations through his chest. His chest brushes my sensitive nipples, and I can't help but squeeze him again.

"Bad girl." He groans as he drags his slick cock through my grip. Despite my tense muscles he slides into me without pain, only pleasure.

"Please, Daniel, please!" I beg as he speeds up his thrusts. I'm helpless to ease his way, spasming on his cock as he sets a brutal pace. Each thrust causing his balls to slap against my ass and his pelvis to brush my clit. Higher and higher I soar as he takes my body and molds it for his pleasure.

His lips slam down onto mine as his thrusts falter and the warm spurt of his seed fills my channel. Before he pulls out, he reaches between our sweat slicked bodies and strokes my clit in calm confident circles until I fall into ecstasy one last time.

Our sweat has dried, cooling our skin by the time he rolls to the side and pulls me into the comforting cradle of his arms. The silence that lingers in the aftermath coats my body like a weighted blanket. My bones feel heavy and my muscles loose as I lay in a melted puddle against my husband.

"I'm going to forgive you for driving your car up the mountain." Daniels words rumble through his chest under my chin.

"Odd thing to say after sex but okay." I reply with a questioning tone.

"I have zero intentions of letting you leave this bed for the foreseeable future."

"Oh?" My coquettish tone draws a smug smile from Daniel's face. Our languid cuddle transforms in an instant when he flips me onto my back and slides down the bed to kneel between my knees.

"Spread your legs, Angel. I need another taste."

Epilogue

Lily

*T*wo *years later*

"Daniel, stop that!" I scold when Daniel's hands slip from my waist down to cup my ass. This man has struggled to be appropriate in public since we were married and when we're alone he can never keep his hands to himself.

Waiting for Daniel to come home from a quick electrical fix at the Jergen's place, I was checking on the chili I set up in the slow cooker this morning, when he came up behind me and got all handsy. Dropping the ladle on the counter, I spin to wrap my husband in a tight hug. It doesn't matter how long or short any job takes him to complete, I miss him just the same.

"I can and will touch my wife whenever I want." He squeezes my ass to underline his point. With my head pressed against his chest he can't see my eye roll or my smile.

"Your mom will be here any minute!" I protest while he works my yellow sundress over my head. Even as I argue I help him unhook my bra.

"Percy will keep her occupied. I guarantee that she over-estimated how easy it is to take care of a toddler." he reminds me as I unbuckle his jeans. He kicks the denim and his boxers off a second later. His flannel shirt and white undershirt join the growing pile of clothes soon after.

"Your mother is punctual-" His lips cover mine cutting off my token protest. With both of us already naked we both know it was only for show anyway.

"Please don't deny me a taste of my favorite girl," he groans as he lifts me up onto the quartz countertop of our kitchen island. My legs are spread before he finishes the plea.

"That's it, Angel, let me see that tight little pussy," he says as he runs a finger through my wet folds. He thrusts two fingers into me coating them in my wetness. Licking them in front of me he sinks to his knees and parts my slit with his tongue lapping at my pussy like a man starved.

"I'm your only girl," I growl while grabbing twin fistfuls of his hair grinding my pussy against his bearded face.

Ever since becoming pregnant I have become more possessive of my husband. Something that has only heightened our pleasure. As I become more possessive, Daniel matches my ferocity leading to easily the best sex of my life.

Pleasure heats my body as he works his tongue first into my slit mimicking the motion of how his cock will fuck me soon and then as he flicks it against my clit. Already a dripping mess, it doesn't take long for me to fall over the edge crying out for more even as I come back to earth.

"My one and only," he whispers with a bright smile. "Forever. I love you, Lily."

"I love you too." I say with a moan as he lines his cock up with my entrance. The head of his cock brushes my clit, and I can feel my heartbeat there. Strong and steady just as the love that has grown between us. A love that if I'm honest started on the sidewalk where we first met face to face. One look at my rugged mountain man and I was a goner.

He slams his cock into me in a single thrust causing my breasts to bounce from the impact.

"Mine," he growls as he thrusts into my wet channel to punctuate the word. It's a claim and a vow that he's made every day since we got married.

"Yours," I answer in turn as he picks up the pace with his thrusts.

"Harder," I command with a gasp.

Never failing to disappoint, he rams into me, and I have to grip the counter to keep from sliding backwards. Each thrust presses his cock against the soft spongy spot at the front of my pussy and it's not long before I'm begging.

"Please oh please-" I cry as I approach the edge.

"Look at you, taking me so well. You always take me so well Angel," he says through gritted teeth.

I'm balanced on the edge. So close to going over with tingles spreading through my body when Daniel leans forward and sucks my nipple into his mouth nipping it gently. With a pulse I go over the edge crying his name and he follows me filling me to the brim with his seed.

"These might be my favorite part of your pregnancy," Daniel says cupping my enlarged breast and thumbing the nipple.

I swat him away with a breathy sigh.

"If you don't want to go for another round keep your hands to yourself," I grumble.

"I'd love to, but I think our alone time is up Angel," he says just as I hear Mary's truck door slam. It's distinct on the mountain with its creaking hinge.

I'm up in a flash grabbing my clothes and dashing to the bedroom. Daniel's booming laugh follows me up the stairs.

I know he'll be dressed in time to greet his mother and our son at the door. They'll chat giving me plenty of time to change into something warmer to match the cooling temperature of the mountain.

My sex drive has been ramped up during both pregnancies. First with Percy and now with our second child on the way. And as warm and loving as Daniel is, the man is not a mind reader. So, when I'm in the mood I change into one of my sundresses and flaunt it around the cabin.

Never fails to get Daniel's cock hard seeing me in those short dresses.

"Lily!" Mary calls when she sees me coming down the stairs. "You look gorgeous."

"Thank you," I say appreciatively.

It's still early in this pregnancy but I'm sure like my first I'll swell up in no time at all. Wouldn't change it for the world though. Not when I see Percy's face peeking up at me from where he's stacking some blocks on the living room rug.

Daniel and I agreed we both wanted a large family and with our two we're well on our way. Watching as he plays with our son showing him how to line up the matching colors and then laughing when River bulldozes them down, I know I made the right choice.

I never doubt my decision about moving to Crescent Ridge. Not when I have such a wonderful man as my husband. But I do miss being closer to my sister, Gloria.

"When is your sister coming up?" Mary asks while we dish out the chili into bowls. I put a small amount into the fridge to cool for Percy while we talk.

"Next week, if her boss lets her have the time off." I reply with excitement.

"Does she not have PTO?" Mary asks between bites.

"No. It's a start up and it's in the early stages. Or so she's been telling me for the last few years," I explain. "She has no benefits."

"She must love that job," Mary says with a raised eyebrow.

I raise my own eyebrows and let my face tell the story on that one. As impulsive as I am, my sister's life runs like clockwork. Getting her to agree to take a week off to visit took two years of convincing to pull off.

And begging.

"She'll love it up here," Daniel says as he carries Percy. "We'll make it so that she'll never want to leave."

As I watch Daniel feed our son, I feel a warm wave of contentment wash over me. Happy tears roll down my face as I look upon my husband. Even if she hates it and never visits again, I know I made the right choice by choosing Daniel. I was always meant to be here on this mountain with this man.

And for the rest of my life, I will be.

The End

Meet Gloria and the mountain man who convinces her to take an impulsive leap for love in Mountain Man's Rescued Mail Order Bride.

You can sign up for my newsletter or follow me on Amazon or Facebook for updates on new releases.

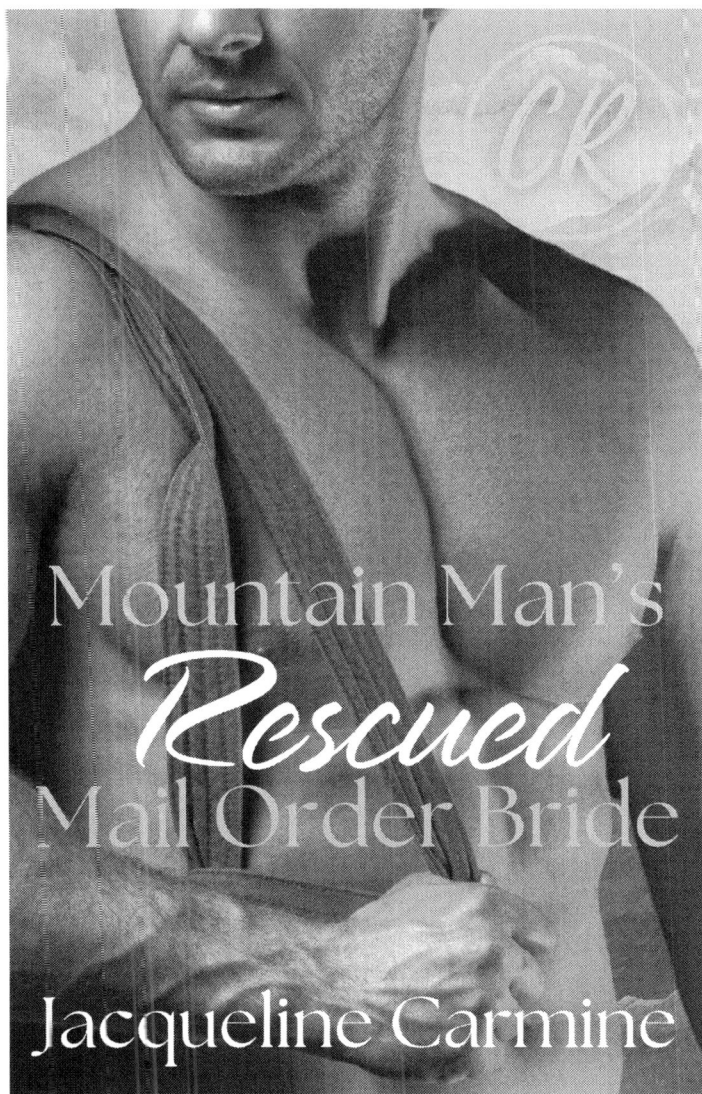

Mountain Man's
Rescued
Mail Order Bride

Jacqueline Carmine

Contents

Shawn

Another day stuck behind the desk filling out reports has my nerves on edge. In a town like Crescent Ridge most days are quiet, but the lull is beginning to feel eerie. No wildfires, irresponsible campers, or even cats stuck in trees. It's too quiet.

No one at the station is going to say it though. Saying the word quiet is the jinx and no one wants a repeat of last summer. The wildfire that decimated twenty percent of the valley was a nightmare. Too much for our local fire station to handle on our own, we had to call in outside reinforcements and volunteers to get the blaze under control.

Now in peak hiking season, we have a lull.

"I want volunteers to cover extra shifts for tonight and the rest of the weekend," the captain's voice rings out and a chorus of groans from my fellow firefighters echo through the room.

"There is a huge storm rolling through and there isn't an empty campsite on the mountain."

I raise my hand along with Bill and Corey. They've had enough experience in past years to know the drill. Mandatory evacuation before the storm hits to ensure everyone makes it safely down from the summit.

Nylon tents don't protect from landslides and downed trees. Stubborn hikers not wanting to give up their weekend retreat or families their yearly vacation ensure that it'll take extra manpower to evacuate the mountain safely.

In other towns and cities, it wouldn't be a job for the fire station to handle. But on the ridge, we're fire and rescue. And we spend more time rescuing stranded hikers than fighting fires.

I never thought it would be my calling but after leaving the military I needed purpose. And space. Buying a mountain cabin was the most impulsive thing I've ever done. But five years out of the service and four since I moved out here to the corner of nowhere and I don't regret it.

"My wife will be baking cupcakes for the volunteers," Captain Thomas adds once he's taken our names down and added us to the roster.

"Awe! Why didn't you lead with that?" one of the rookies called out and I couldn't smother a chuckle.

"Rookie mistake!" Bill yells back.

It never fails that the captain's wife Melody makes desserts for those on voluntary overtime. And while her famous strawberry lemonade cupcakes are tempting enough to have Bill raise his hand, I volunteered because of that uneasy feeling rolling around in my stomach.

Like the thunder before a storm, my nerves are warning me something is coming.

Gloria

I love my sister. Hand on heart, swear on my soul. But staying with her and her family is going to drive me over the edge. I loved meeting my nephew, Percy is the greatest child of all time. But he is a toddler, and my sister has her hands full being a mom. And when she isn't in mom mode, she and Daniel are attached at the hip. Their romance is sweet enough to make my teeth ache.

"Get out of here." Lily's words hit me hard before she saw the expression on my face.

"Not like that! God, mom brain much?" she asks pacing the room as she comforts Percy. "I meant see the town. Get dinner or check out the bookshop."

I want to go. Desperately. But part of the reason I finally agreed to take a vacation was to help my sister. I may not have much experience with children, especially toddlers, but I knew she would need extra support near the end of her second pregnancy. A week isn't much, but I wanted to show up for my sister. I want her to know that I'm just a call away if she needs me. And if she needs me, I will be there.

"Do something for yourself on this vacation, Gloria." Lily's voice is stern in a way I've never heard. Maybe it comes with motherhood.

"Are you sure?" the small pinch of guilt makes me ask. I've done the laundry and dishes and even meal prepped for Lily and her little family. It doesn't feel like enough. Two years without visiting leaves me feeling off centered like I have a debt to repay.

"Go! And bring me back something from *Sugar Crossing*. Something chocolatey," Lily orders with a smile. The blue eyes we share are framed by her oval glasses and I can see the genuine warmth within.

And with that I slip on my sneakers, and grab my wallet, phone, and keys before I dash out to my car. I'll finish my penance later.

For now, I want to see more of this mountain and the town that calls it home. Lily and I grew up in the city and unlike my sister I've never ventured far from our home roots.

I'm halfway to town when I see signs for the summit trailhead. I've been inside Lily's cabin all week and all I really want to do is stretch my legs. Feel that fresh mountain air on my face.

Pulling into the small dirt parking lot surrounded by pine trees, I'm a little surprised to be the only one here. But I quickly reason that experienced hikers start their hike closer to the mountain base. I'm not that far from the cabin and I know they live close to the summit. There's a sign posted near the trail with a map and fun facts about the area, like the types of trees and flora common to the area. It also has a time estimate for hiking the trail. Checking the time on my phone I see that I have plenty of time to make it to the summit and back before dark.

I can stop at any bookstore or any pastry shop in the city. It's the scenery that isn't going to be there when I get back home. Once I'm done with the trail, I can swing by the bakery and get my sister something special as a thank you.

I grab my travel tumbler and check that it has water. I already have my sneakers on, and my clothes are light enough for a little hiking. Soft cotton tee and some leggings never wronged anyone.

Setting out on the trail it's easy to see why my sister and brother-in-law chose to live out here.

There is a serene kind of quiet out here. A stillness that draws my attention to the trees and plants around me. The softness of the dirt under my shoes and the cool breeze blowing through the forest.

I did expect there to be more birds but it's a beautiful place even without their chirping.

Shawn

The lull was a fluke.

The storm rolled in earlier than expected to the surprise of no one at the station. Evacuating the campsites was mildly troubling but as the rainfall increased and lightning cracked across the sky it became easier and easier to escort campers down the mountain.

Just as the last camper from Campsite D pulls their van out to follow Bill's truck down the mountain the radio crackles and a call from the station comes in.

"Langley, there is a hiker stranded at the summit trailhead. Peters saw the car on his way down from Campsite B and it matches the description of Hart's sister-in-law. They called down to the station when she didn't return to their cabin a few hours ago," dispatch says.

"Copy. I'll check on it," I answer before backing my truck out of the campsite parking lot and beginning the slow climb up to the trailhead.

The rain has already made the road winding up the mountain slick and I have no doubt that the dirt parking lot at the trailhead is a muddy pit by now.

Parking as close to the road as I dare, I grab my flashlight and make my way over to the lone silver car in the lot. Sure enough, there is no sister-in-law to be found. Either she caught a ride out or she's still on the trail in the dark and the rain.

When I heard about Daniel's success with Pearl's Matchmaking, I was inspired to create my own profile. But after weeks of stilted conversations and now this I don't see myself finding a bride any time soon. Lily is a sweetheart. But if wandering kin are part of the package, I might just commit to being single.

I curse myself for not asking for a name as I begin walking the trail.

"Hello?" I call out. "Lily's sister! Can you hear me?"

Several minutes pass as I follow the trail, keeping an eye out for anything manmade.

"Fire and rescue!" I eventually called out.

I don't know how to address her and at least this way she knows I'm not a threat. Hopefully, she has a light and didn't wander off the trail. If she is lost, it'll be nearly impossible to track her in this storm. The sheer drops and ravines that she could stumble upon in the dark make it urgent that I find her quickly.

If she's on this trail she is lucky.

She's lucky that Corey noticed her car, considering we cleared this lot earlier in the day. She's lucky that Daniel trusted his gut and called in her disappearance. In the city she wouldn't be considered missing until twenty-four hours passed. But on the ridge, we do things a little differently. If the loved ones are worried, we take it seriously.

"Hello!" I call out after a few more minutes.

I almost don't catch the answering, "Hello!" over the sound of the rain and thunder.

Over the next rise I see a dim light shining on the ground before it briefly rises to scan for me. I raise my own flashlight and wave it back and forth.

She's using her phone for a light. Not the best but better than nothing. As she walks down the slope, slipping on the mud, she slowly comes into the light of my flashlight. Every word I prepped leaves my head. Every protocol and every safety lecture just gone.

Her brown hair is down and plastered to her scalp. The biggest blue eyes I've ever seen are looking at me like I've hung the moon and it's enough to knock me senseless. The thin T-shirt she's wearing is soaked through clinging to her curves and I can see goosebumps on the tan skin not covered by the shirt. Even if I didn't see her trembling, I would know she's cold.

Without a word I take off my windbreaker and hand it to her. Both of us will be soaked to the bone now but I have no idea how long she's been out in the storm. She could very well be in the beginning stages of hypothermia. Waiting for her to pull the jacket on gives me time to sort my thoughts and introduce myself.

"Shawn Langley. I'm with Crescent Ridge fire and rescue. Your brother-in-law called in your disappearance."

She nods in response but otherwise she doesn't acknowledge me. Best to get her out of the rain and back to Daniel's cabin in a hurry.

I begin to lead her back down the trail, but I come up short when her hand strikes out and grabs the back of my shirt. Her blue eyes are wide with terror.

"There is a man," she says and I begin scanning our surroundings. It wouldn't be difficult to sneak up on us in the dark. I *need* to get her back to safety.

"We need to hurry," I say. The sense of urgency makes my voice lower, nearly a growl.

But when I grab her arm to usher her down the trail she resists while shaking her head. Her pale pink lips tremble as she speaks.

"No." Watching her sway in the freezing wind ripping its way through the trees has me on the verge of throwing her over my shoulder and carrying her back to the truck. It's the determined look that comes over her face that keeps me from following through with the urge. "He needs help. He scared me but he didn't hurt me."

With those words she turns to lead me back up the rise she just slid down. Nothing is adding up. She was terrified when I found her. Scared of the man, not the storm.

"I need to get you to safety first," I argue, planting my feet.

"You won't find him without me," she argues right back. There is a fierce gleam shining in her wide eyes as she glares back at me. "I hit him with a rock. He's unconscious and he's hurt. He needs help and that's your job, right?"

Her sharp tone gets my feet moving and I let her tug me forward.

"You hit him with a rock?" I ask as we climb the rise.

"Yes. I thought he was a bear," she says calmly, like she's not admitting to an assault charge.

"Did he attempt to harm you?" I ask just to cover my bases. Maybe she could argue self-defense.

"At the time I thought so," she answers in a low mumble. I can barely hear her over the wind. "But I'm not so sure now. I was pretty scared, and he came out of nowhere, yelling at me and I panicked."

I fight back a groan. There is only one man she could have met. Only Jeb lives close enough and is crazy enough to be out in this storm. I can only hope she didn't kill him. It would be hard as hell to date a woman in prison.

Watching her hips sway in front of me as she leads me back to the site of the accident has the front of my pants feeling tight despite the chill in the air. Grateful for her attention being elsewhere, I adjust the growing erection and pin it in place with the waistband of my pants. I don't need her seeing me like this. She's having the worst night of her life.

Just over the rise I can see the prone form of a man lying face down on the trail. He's massive. And I would know him from a mile away. There are a lot of men who make this mountain their home. I'm one of them. But Jeb is the only one who wears fur and lives entirely off the grid.

With the deer hides and raccoon cap I can see why she thought he was a bear. Especially in the dark.

As I approach, he starts to gain consciousness. Grumbling and groaning as he rises unsteadily to his feet.

"Jeb." I call out as he shakes his head like he's trying to shake himself awake.

"Shawn?" he calls out and as I get closer, I can see him squinting at the woman standing behind me. "You need to keep an eye on that one."

With a grumble he turns to leave but the woman darts forward to stop him.

"Wait!" she shouts. "You're hurt, and you need to go to the hospital. You might have a concussion."

He glances over his shoulder at her, and I swear beneath his overgrown beard the beast actually smiles.

"Don't worry about me. Not the first time I've been mistaken for a bear. At least you didn't shoot me like that one hunter did."

She watches as he disappears into the brush.

"I'm sorry but I didn't get your name," I say when she finally accepts that Jeb isn't going to seek help.

"Gloria Porter," she says shortly as she falls into step with me. "You're a first responder. You should have looked at his head. I hit him pretty hard."

"Trust me, Gloria, he's got a hard head. He'll be fine," I reply shaking my head. This isn't my first run in with Jeb. I know that pushing him to let me check his head would only get me a matching lump on my own head for my trouble. She's lucky it was him. Another man might have pressed charges. But Jeb was just impressed that she got the jump on him.

The man has a funny way at looking at life.

I can see her fidgeting with the sleeves of my jacket in my peripheral vision and I just know she isn't satisfied with my answer. The urge to reassure her is instant.

"He was shot last year by a poacher. He dug the bullet out, cleaned and dressed the wound by himself. Trust me, it'll take more than a little slip like you to send him to his maker."

Gloria is silent as we make good time back to the trail-head, but I can practically hear her thoughts simmering away.

"Thank you for your help," she says while approaching her car. The tires are sunk several inches into the mud, but she hasn't noticed that yet. I doubt it's going to move but it might if it's light enough. I linger under the cover of the nearby pine trees as she starts her car and attempts to back out.

The tires spin and sling mud as the car just sinks deeper. I wait until she gives up, her forehead falling forward to rest on the steering wheel before I approach her car window.

Less than an hour in her company and I can tell she has a lot of pride in her independence. Even if I hadn't shown up to help her, she would've made it back to her car. If she didn't have a cell signal, she could have slept in it overnight and walked until she found a signal in the morning.

But I am here and I'm not going to leave her stranded. And it's not just because it's my job to clear this mountain. There's something pulling me to Gloria. Something that has all my attention on her.

Her dark head jerks up when I gently knock on the window with my knuckles. I try to give her a reassuring smile as her blue eyes fill with tears.

"I don't have the equipment to pull you out on this truck, but I can run you up to Daniel's cabin. We can get you unstuck tomorrow."

"Thank you," she says as she follows me back to my truck. I call dispatch and let them know I've found Gloria and that the summit trail is clear.

She's drenched from the rain and shaking like a leaf as the adrenaline leaves her body. I have half a mind to take her down the mountain to see the local doctor. But the logical part of my brain kicks in, telling me I'm being overly cautious. I begin following the windy path up the mountain as the truck's heater slowly warms the cab.

I spend more of the drive up the mountain thinking of how to ask Gloria on a date than I'd like to admit.

"How long have you been in fire and rescue?" Gloria asks after a few moments.

"Four years," I say while mentally cursing myself for not being better at small talk. The last thing I want to talk about is my job. I'd rather learn more about her. Her favorite foods, hobbies, and exactly how attached she is to living in the city.

Mail order brides are growing in popularity around the ridge. Mostly because of Daniel's success but also because it's difficult to find women who want to uproot their lives to live in a rural town. Or on a literal mountain in my case.

"Lily mentioned you work for a tech startup," I say hoping she'll do the lion's share of talking.

"Well, it's not a startup anymore. It's finally gaining momentum and the apps we're developing are growing in popularity. It's mostly health apps now but I don't think you would need them living out here. Our users tend to be office workers who lead a sedentary lifestyle and need the push to get active."

"No, I get my fair share of exercise," I agree. Hard not to with my job.

I'm about to ask her if she's been to Lefty's diner when I pull around a curve and find a large tree blocking the road. Even if I had the equipment to drag it, the tree would be too big. It'll have to be cut into manageable pieces.

"Damn it!" Gloria's shout fills the truck cab.

I empathize with her frustration, but I push it down. Anger never makes a situation better. Especially not when fate has its hands around your throat.

Picking up the radio to call dispatch again, I'm not surprised when they tell me that they can't get to it tonight. It's not the only downed tree that's been reported and there are several people in town without power. The blocked road is a nuisance but the trees causing outages in town take precedent.

"Langley, the road is blocked on our end too," dispatch calls out another road blockage near the town and I fight the urge to pump my fist into the air. There is only one road up the mountain and road blockages on both sides mean one thing.

"Langley signing off," I reply to dispatch.

"Copy that," dispatch replies. "We'll message when the road is cleared."

I catch Gloria's wide-eyed stare and hasten to reassure her.

"Don't worry. The roads will be cleared in the morning, and you can stay at my cabin until I can drive you back to your sister's."

The jinx might be in full effect, but luck is on my side this once. Situated between the road blockages are several cabins. Each spaced well apart. And one of them is mine.

Gloria is coming home with me.

Gloria

I'm in big trouble.

My day went to shit the moment I started hiking that trail. Ninety percent of it's my fault. I misread the sign and misjudged the time it would take to hike the trail. I didn't turn back when the sky turned grey. In fact, since I believed I was close to the summit I didn't turn back until the rain came pouring down.

Then the sun set, taking the last bit of the day's warmth with it. I was left cold and wet in the dark with only my phone's flashlight to see the trail. Then Jeb scared the living daylights out of me.

But then Shawn appeared with his bright smile and his deep voice, telling me I was safe. The blonde giant with his broad chest and piercing blue eyes had me stammering like a preteen girl with her first crush. I stared for entirely too long to be appropriate.

To say that my day did a complete one eighty is the least of it. I could feel his stare on my ass the entire way back to where I struck Jeb. Jeb, the mountain man who apparently likes cosplaying as a bear.

When we found the road blocked by that tree my frustration was real. That one more obstacle would prevent me from getting back to my sister and a hot shower was almost more than I could endure. The cherry to top my shitty sundae.

The news that the town was also inaccessible almost made me cry. I already look like a drowned rat with my hair sticking to my skin like wet paper and my mascara running. Waterproof my ass. Looking like a wet rat is not the first impression I want to make with a man as hot as Shawn. The longer we spend together while I look like *this* only feeds my temper.

But then Shawn told me he lived nearby, somewhere between the fallen trees. A night spent with the most gorgeous guy I have ever seen was not on my bingo card for this year. Suddenly I had to feign my frustration. If I revealed how happy I was to be stuck in close quarters with this mouthwatering mountain man, he would think I was insane. I might look ragged now, but I can turn this around.

"You know your sister and Daniel's success has led to most of the men in Crescent Ridge signing up for Pearl's Matchmaking?" Shawn asks.

I should be proud that my sister is inspiring the town but all I feel now is a sick twisting in my stomach.

"Including you?" I ask in return, trying not to let the jealousy color my tone.

"I signed up months ago, but it hasn't worked out for me. Now I'm certain that's not how I'm going to find my wife." His gaze is locked on the road but for a split second he glances my way with enough heat to warm me up despite the lingering chill from the storm. "Did you sign up to be a bride like your sister?"

I want to lie and say yes.

"No," I say with a small shake of my head. "Lily is the impulsive one. That hike was the most impulsive thing I've done in a long time. And look how that turned out. I always like having a well thought out plan."

Or I used to. Now as I'm considering my options every choice seems more impulsive than what my sister did to meet her husband. Lily and Daniel wrote letters to each other before marrying. Their courtship took weeks which at the time seemed crazy fast to me. But I'm hooked on the idea of claiming Shawn. I've known the man less than an hour. I've surpassed my sister's impulsivity by a mile.

On the way back to my sister's, before we found the road blocked, I was planning out the rest of the weekend. I was going to bake a batch of brownies as a thank you and bring them down to the station. Naturally, I was going to be wearing nicer clothes and have a fresh coat of mascara on when I did so. And I was going to flirt until I got Shawn's number and a date if it killed me.

"It's not much," Shawn says as we turn down a long gravel driveway. "But it's got hot water and internet."

I was sold when it was just me and him in a cabin alone. At this point he's overselling it. But I'm not going to tell him that.

"I'm just happy to get out of the rain," I tell him as he parks the truck in front of his cabin.

In the darkness I can't see much besides the large front porch.

"I wasn't expecting company, so I'm sorry for the mess," Shawn says as he leads me to the front door.

As clean as his work truck is I doubt his home is that messy. When he opens the door and lets me into his home, I realize I couldn't be more wrong.

"It's bad. I know," Shawn says as he closes the door behind us. "I never really finished moving in."

Boxes everywhere. Stacks of books are leaning haphazardly amongst loose papers on the floor, and I count not one but three totes sitting by a nearby bookshelf. An empty bookshelf. The man has dozens of books sitting on his floor and not even one on the shelf.

His truck was so clean I worried over my muddy sneakers staining his floorboards. But this is his home. His messy, trainwreck home.

"When did you move?" I ask as Shawn leads me down a hallway to a bathroom. He's showing me where all the towels and soaps are when my question causes a sheepish expression to cross his face. The bright red color highlighting his cheeks makes me feel giddy.

"Four years ago," He mumbles before excusing himself. "Leave your wet clothes and I'll wash them for you. I'll leave a change of clothes outside the door for you to change into."

As I shower, I can't help but imagine the life I could have here. Hunky mountain man aside I would be closer to my sister. I didn't realize how much I missed having her close until I came out here. Every year I'm missing milestones in her life. And now with Percy I'm missing out every month as he grows. If I live the rest of my life in the city how often will I be able to see them? Life is passing me by and I'm tired of missing out.

With my work as a software developer, I could get a job working remotely. It won't pay as well, I'm sure. But I can't ignore this longing. And if moving closer brings me into Shawn's orbit, who am I to complain? I could be the woman making his cabin into a home. The woman warming his bed and his cock.

Wet hands slide down my body with ease. Stroking my nipples before trailing down to tease my clit. I try to be quiet as I slip my fingers between my folds, thrusting into my core. A low moan escapes when I rub circles around my clit, and I come in a wave of heat and bliss. A part of me wants Shawn to hear. Wants him to want me as much as I want him.

Shawn

My joy is tinted with guilt. A good man would never be happy that a woman is stranded. But I've never considered myself a good man. Not truly. I didn't serve my country out of the goodness of my heart. I sought glory selfishly and I paid the price for my vanity.

I change into a pair of sweatpants and a shirt before gathering an old shirt and pair of shorts for Gloria to wear after her shower. Envisioning her in my bed with sleep rumpled hair and wearing nothing but my shirt has my cock stirring.

Feeling like a jerk for fantasizing about a vulnerable woman I know I can't pursue anything physical. Despite the attraction we both feel I won't act on it. Not until the road is clear and Gloria can reject me comfortably.

I will use the time fate has provided to grow our connection and build the foundation for a relationship. I can't lock her away and keep her from going back to her life in the city. No matter how much I want to.

Placing the clothing beside the bathroom door, I turn towards the kitchen just as a low moan reaches my ears. Fighting with myself I lean closer to the door and just over the sound of the shower I can hear her breathy little moans.

My cock goes stiff in my sweats.

The sounds she's making have me on edge. All I can imagine is Gloria spread out on my bed moaning as I drive my cock into her wet pussy. Fisting my cock through my sweats provides me no relief but I can't risk being caught with my pants down. I don't want her to think I'm creepy.

Even if I am.

Another moan hits my ears, and my imagination runs wild. My hand slips down my sweats to grip my cock. Sliding my hand up and down as I picture her in the shower.

The warm water gliding over her skin. Her slim fingers massaging soapy tits before trailing down to finger herself. The delicate arch of her neck as she leans back into the spray. Her luscious curves jiggling as she shimmies with need. Her fingers too short to reach the spot she needs. My fingers would reach. I could make her come on my hand while sucking on her rosy nipples.

My hand speeds up as I picture her coming with her cheeks the same shade of pink as her nipples and my name on her lips. I choke back a moan when I come. I allow myself a single moment to lean my forehead against the door before I leave.

The shower has gone quiet, and I need to change into a fresh pair of pants. The only thing worse than being caught outside the door would be for her to see the stain my seed leaves on the fabric.

Gloria

The worn cotton of my borrowed shirt is soft against my overheated skin. The shorts Shawn provided cling tightly to my waist but hang loosely around my thighs. I look entirely too much like a child for my liking. The clothing only serves to add to the feeling of helplessness that's been building since I realized that I was in trouble on the trail.

I knew better than to risk hiking after dark. Common sense says I should have checked the weather report before I went out. I didn't even tell my sister that I was going on a hike.

I could've met anyone on that trail. Meeting Jeb was bad enough, and he had the best intentions when he found me.

Walking down the hallway that leads to the main living area of the cabin I find myself walking a bit faster to get off the cold hardwood and onto the plush carpet I saw when we came in from the storm. Back home in my apartment I wear socks all day just to have a layer between the soles of my feet and the chilly vinyl flooring.

Just as I reach the living room, I hear a crash. Changing direction, I go around the wall separating the two areas to see Shawn's predicament. The spicy scent of chili hits my nose and I spot the slow cooker sitting on the counter. A ladle covered in chili lies on the hardwood floor while Shawn holds a bowl filled to the brim with chili in both his left hand and his right while pinning the glass lid of the slow cooker against the bottom cabinets with his hip.

"Help," he says with his bottom lip tucked under upper lip and a mild look of panic in his eyes.

Stepping forward I save the glass lid and replace it on the appliance before taking one of the bowls from Shawn.

While I take a seat at his kitchen table Shawn goes to the fridge to grab our drinks before joining me

"Thank you," I say while lifting the bowl slightly.

"No problem, I thought a warm meal would do wonders after being out in that storm for so long.".

"Yeah, I was pretty dumb."

"Don't say that."

"I knew better," I argue as I spoon a healthy bite of chili into my mouth.

"You weren't prepared. It happens," Shawn replies with a shrug. "But you kept your cool. You stayed on the trail and used your resources. And when you thought you were being attacked you were able to defend yourself."

I chew my food while I watch him take a drink from his beer.

"I get a lot of calls for stranded hikers, Gloria." His blue eyes shine with something I can't name. "You're probably the only person who has gotten the jump on Jeb. The man is built like a house and meaner than any grizzly."

Just as I start to protest his defense of me, he holds up a hand and with a wide smile says, "You're not going to convince me that you're not a badass. Sorry."

"I got lucky," I say with a matching smile. His teasing nature is infectious.

"The more you talk, the more I'm convinced that you lured poor Jeb out onto that trail. It was all a ploy," Shawn says finishing the last of his chili.

"Stop," I reply. My cheeks feel sunburnt from smiling so hard.

"I'm just glad that I found you," he says while looking at me with an intensity that has me hooked.

"Me too," I say. "I didn't want to be stuck out there."

"No, of course not," he says fiddling with his spoon. "But I meant that I was glad that *I* got the call rather than one of my coworkers. One of the other guys."

It takes me a minute to gather his meaning. And then, all I can say-all I can think is-

"Oh."

A silent beat and then his gaze drops from mine.

"I'm sorry. I didn't mean to make you uncomfortable."

"You didn't," I insist. I can see that he doesn't believe me but that's fine. Now I know we're on the same page. The attraction I feel isn't one sided. He's in this bubble of anticipation with me.

"I would've swiped right on you," I blurt out before I can filter my words.

Does he even have a dating profile? Or is that useless in a small town like Crescent Ridge?

"That's the good one, right?" he asks with a smile, laughter dancing in his eyes.

"Yeah."

"Would you like to have dinner with me? In a day or two once the road is clear, I mean."

I nod and I can see the tension leave his shoulders. He's taking our bowls to the sink, and he has his back to me when I just can't help myself. Maybe anticipation would make it sweeter. The heart would grow fonder. But I know exactly what I want. And I've wanted Shawn since we met on that trail.

"I want you to fuck me."

The dishes clatter into the sink and I'm sure one of the bowls broke. I step behind him and reach around to palm

his cock through his sweatpants. The hard length is warm to the touch even through the fabric.

Shawn

The darkening desire in her deep blue eyes calls to me in a way that I've never felt before. Already blood is rushing to my cock where it is straining against the front of my sweatpants.

Her gentle touch, even through the thick fabric, has me wanting to throw her down and make her scream my name. She squeezes me softly guiding her hand slowly along the outline of my cock and I would give anything to feel her bare skin on mine. Whether I've spoken my thoughts aloud or she is on the same wavelength I don't know. All I know is that when she pulls the band down and grabs my swollen cock I want to come. On her, in her, everywhere.

But first.

"Come here, Sweet," I say grabbing her hand that's wrapped around my cock. She pouts with her pretty pink bottom lip sticking out. The demon inside me wants to suck it into my mouth and bite until it's as red as her fingernails. A mark that warns other men away. A mark that shows she's mine.

Leading her into my bedroom I don't let her take in the décor. She's already seen the chaos that is my home. Gloria doesn't need to see the unmade bed and piles of books that have taken over my nightstand.

A firm hand on her shoulder has her sitting on the edge of the bed and a gentle press of my fingers to her collarbone has her laying back. Her damp brunette curls spread wild around her head like a halo while she eyes me with blatant hunger.

This is where she belongs. Not in some tiny, cookie cutter apartment washed in white and grey in the city. She belongs in my cabin, in my bed, and under me. In nature wild and free with color blooming all around her with a smile on her face and fire in her eyes. She belongs with me.

If it takes the rest of my life, I'll convince her.

Pushing up the frayed edge of my old T-shirt I let her borrow I trail kisses across her soft stomach. I nip her sides until she's squirming beneath me with laughter.

"It tickles!" she shrieks.

Flipping up the shirt I expose her bare breasts tipped with rosy nipples the same shade as her lips. I flick one with the tip of my tongue and she stops laughing. Rolling the other between my thumb and finger I lick and lap at the peak until she arches beneath me.

"Shawn-I need more," she moans as I give her a gentle nibble.

When I pull back the nipple is the same shade of red I pictured her lips. Returning my attention to the other, I snake my free hand under the band of her shorts. Easing my finger into her slick heat I'm not surprised when she grips my finger and tenses underneath me. The arch of her neck pulsing as she strains against me.

"You look so pretty when you come."

"Bet I'll look even better on your cock." Her impish smirk is back as she grips me by my shirt and pulls me up the bed. I follow her without thought. The sight of her flush with pleasure, breasts heaving, rosy cheeked, and eyes bright has me in her thrall.

She could ask anything of me, and I would happily oblige. That she wants this, us, as much as I do is my undoing.

"You're so fucking perfect," I moan before I kiss her.

Our last first kiss is everything. Her tongue is slick against mine painting me with her warmth and her passion as the kiss goes on and on. Hips rising, she brushes against me, and I don't hesitate to push down and grind my cock into her.

"Naked," she says breaking our kiss. "Now." Wrenching my shirt up my body she pulls it over my head before I can catch up. Arms tangling in the sleeves I laugh at her eagerness.

"We have all night," I say before leaning down to kiss her again.

"Shawn. If you don't hurry up and fuck me-" I interrupt her rant with another kiss.

Sliding my sweatpants down and helping her out of her shorts I don't give her time to complain before my body is covering hers. Every one of her soft curves molds around my hard body and I love the way they jiggle when she moves.

"Shawn," her moan is low as I kiss and nip at every exposed inch. Leaving a trail of red marks on my way down to her heated core I can't help but moan when her sharp little nails scratch my scalp.

My eyes meet hers as I slide down her body and I don't look away as I part her folds and let my tongue slide through her warmth. Her sweet taste coats my tongue as I drink from her. Pupils blown wide I keep my gaze on her as I lick my way to her clit. Every reaction that I notice changes my approach. When her breath hitches, I know I've found what she likes.

Slow circles around her clit. Never touching it directly, she likes to be teased. Broad strokes of my tongue through her folds with intermittent thrusts into her core.

I watch as she falls apart again, her orgasm soaking my face and leaving me with a throbbing cock. I can't wait anymore.

Gloria

Two orgasms and already I'm ruined. Spoiled to the ninth degree. This man is never getting rid of me. Watching him work my body into a fever pitch will always be ingrained into my brain. The man is a gift and I'm a greedy bitch.

His cock slides into me easily, coming twice has left me drenched. I don't think I can reach the same peak as before, but I'll be damned if I don't want to try. His muscles flex as he builds a rhythm and I'm hypnotized by the way he moves. For every inch of my softness, he's hard and unyielding. The steamy look in his stormy blue eyes has me melting beneath him.

"More," I beg on a broken whisper as the heat inside me builds. "I need more."

The man knows exactly what I need because he immediately changes the angle. His cock rubs against the front of my walls with every thrust and my needs builds to an incredible crescendo.

"Faster," I order as I sink my nails into his back.

"Good God, do you look good on my cock," Shawns says with gritted teeth. "Take it Sweet. Take it all."

With a rush I feel my blood pounding into my ears and tingles race down my spine as I fall over the edge for the third time. One thrust, then two and Shawn is following me. Warm pulses fill me, and I wrap my arms around his neck to pull him down onto me.

We lay in a contented pile for a bit. The cool dark room and the rhythmic patter of rain hitting the window and roof lulling me into a light sleep. I wake up briefly when Shawn's warmth leaves me, but once he returns with a damp cloth to clean us, I relax back into the bedding.

When he returns to spoon his body around mine, I fall back asleep and don't wake up until I hear a loud banging sound echoing throughout the cabin.

Shawn sits up, blankets pooling at his waist with his blonde hair sticking up in a wild disarray and his blue eyes wide from being startled awake.

"Gloria!" I hear my sister Lily call from the front door.

Shawn and I look at each other and then we're up in a dash throwing clothes at each other. My clothes are still in the dryer, and I don't want to risk walking past one of the large windows to get to the laundry.

"Shawn!" Daniel's deep voice booms when we don't answer his wife's call. "Open the damn door before I kick it down!"

"Give me a minute you overgrown bastard!" Shawn hollers in response and I can't stop the giggle that bubbles up.

Shawn turns to me with an exasperated look, and I tell him between laughs, "We're like a couple of teenagers who got caught necking in a parked car."

His frown stretches into a smile, and it takes Daniel banging on the door with another threat to get us moving again.

"You know some people like to sleep in past dawn," Shawn says, opening the door.

Lily pushes past him with Percy wrapped in a sling across her chest.

"Gloria!" she shouts before she wraps me in her arms as tightly as she can with her son between us. "We were so worried about you."

"I'm sorry, Lily. I thought I had enough time and you're always talking about how beautiful it is out here." Guilt overwhelms me as I try to explain, "The storm rolled in so fast."

"These mountains can be dangerous," Daniel's gruff voice cuts through Lily's sobs before he gentles his tone.

"Just give us a head's up next time. We thought you might have driven over the edge in the storm."

"Daniel's dad died that way," Lily whispers to me.

"I'll always keep you updated from now on," I promise my sister and her husband.

I'm at a loss for what to say when Daniel clears his throat and sweeps his hand out to indicate my attire.

"So, I guess you'll be staying on the mountain then?" he asks with raised eyebrows and a smug smile he aims at his wife.

I start to tell him that Shawn let me borrow his clothes but then I glance down and realize that my shirt is on backwards and the shorts I thought I slipped on are actually Shawn's boxers.

My cheeks burn with embarrassment at being caught red handed. This is *not* how you introduce a man to your family.

"We'll talk about this later," Shawn says before I can tiptoe my way around the verbal landmine my traitorous brother-in-law planted. "Gloria hasn't had breakfast yet."

Shawn

Somehow, I end up with Daniel sitting at my kitchen table drinking coffee from one of my mugs instead of Gloria. Lily had whisked Gloria away to her cabin to change clothes and then the women planned to bring breakfast back to us. I would've pointed out the paper-thin attempt at getting her sister alone for interrogation if I didn't have a soft spot for Lily.

Daniel and I have been friends for years. Always a stand-up fun guy to be around if a tad on the serious side. But when Lily blew into his life like a whirlwind, she softened him and brought out a warmth I'd never seen before.

"You're going to need more than shitty coffee to keep my sister-in-law on this mountain."

"I've got this," I say with a dismissive hand wave. Gloria already agreed to a dinner date, and she didn't seem too happy to have our morning interrupted by her family either. Personally, I would've liked to wake her up in the same manner we went to sleep.

"Finding the two of you together this morning gave Lily hope. Fuck this up for my wife and I'll bury you," Daniel's eyes are dark as he does his best to appear intimidating from his seat at the table.

It might've worked on a different man, but he's learned nothing in the last four years if he thinks he can unsettle me. But since we're making empty threats, I might as well goad Daniel's pride a bit.

"I think I'll have Corey be my best man," I say while pouring my own cup of joe. "He was the one who spotted Gloria's car and led to us meeting."

We both know Corey is a great guy, but it would be weird to ask him to stand beside me when I get married. Especially since Gloria is going to want her sister at her side during the ceremony.

I hide a grimace as the bitter brew coats my tongue. That *is* shitty coffee.

"She wouldn't be within miles of this mountain if I hadn't married Lily. If you make Corey your best man, I'll teach your children to call you Pawpaw instead of Dad."

"You wouldn't."

"And I'll make sure the Anderson sisters get served wine at your reception. Those old gals love a good party."

We both shudder at the memory of the harvest festival last year. One of the lumberjack wives had experimented with a home brew and since she only had the men at the yard as taste testers it had turned out exceptionally strong. Everyone but the lumberjacks and the Anderson sisters, Betty and Barb, had politely sipped from their cups and poured the rest on the ground out of sight.

And that's when things became *interesting*.

I don't think Billy's mustache will ever grow back and the sisters are permanently banned from the local tavern. A feat no other local has ever managed.

"You can be my best man but no more protective big brother jokes," I finally say when I shake the images of Barb dancing on the roof of the funnel cake stand from my head. The woman is in her *sixties*.

"Deal," he says before dumping the rest of his coffee down my kitchen sink. "But on a serious note you need to learn how to make coffee."

Gloria

"But you're only here for the rest of the weekend," Lily says when I tell her I agreed to a dinner date with Shawn. "What if it goes well? Can you handle a long-distance relationship?"

"I'm extending my vacation. And I need the number for that mail order bride agency you used," I say as Lily chops an onion.

"But Shawn's so nice!" she says spinning on her heel to fix me with a bewildered look.

"He's a lot more than nice. That's why I need the number," I say, trying to ignore my sister's withering glare.

"Why?" she asks cocking her hip against the counter and waving the knife in her hand in a *go on* gesture. I wait in silence until she sighs and whips out her own phone and gives me the number.

"He's got a profile," I say as I punch the number into my cell.

"They won't let you take it down. I'm sure if you talked to him, he would take it down. The way he looked at you reminded me of how Daniel looked at me when we first met," Lily says. Content with my answer she resumes her assault on the onion before turning her knife to the poor green bell pepper that's next in line.

"Right before you introduced yourself as his wife to his own mother?" I ask with an arched eyebrow. Mary, Daniel's mother, had stopped by several times during the week I was there, and she had delighted in telling me the story. We both laughed while Lily's blush grew darker and darker.

"And I don't want to take it down I want to make one and have them match us," I say saving the number to call a bit later.

"You want to get married? Just like that? Miss independent?" Lily gives me a skeptical look as I nod and grab a skillet and begin melting a bit of butter to coat the bottom. She's silent as we work in tandem to make a scrambled egg hash, toast, and a plate of waffles. Apparently, Daniel loves them more than life itself.

"It worked for you and Daniel," I finally say while washing the bowl that Lily used for mixing the eggs. "I didn't believe it was possible for me. But when you know, you know."

"Do you love him? Cause he's a great guy and if you're not sure it'll break his heart," she says grabbing the serving dishes and carrying them out to the car while I grab Percy from his bassinet. "Are you sure what you're feeling isn't just relief and gratitude that he saved you?"

"It's far more than gratitude, Lily. But I'm not telling you before I tell him. And if I don't do this, if I don't go after Shawn with everything I've got, it'll break my own heart." Joining my sister in her truck we make our way back down the mountain towards Shawn's cabin and the smallest doubts began to creep into my mind.

My sister, the queen of impulsivity and go with the flow, thinks I'm jumping into the deep end. The overnight bag I packed suddenly feels presumptuous.

If I'm honest with myself, it is a little over the top but if he's not interested in me staying the night then I won't need to call the matchmaking service. The man is signed up for a service looking for a wife, and I'll be damned if he gets matched to anyone else before considering me.

I may have had a bumpy start out here, but I can do anything I set my mind to. If my sister can live out here, then so can I. Us city girls stick together.

Shawn

"Did your sister have to pull the details from under your fingernails or did you break immediately?" I ask Gloria as she hands me several covered dishes. Presumably, the breakfast they *had* to cook at Lily's cabin.

"Judging by the smug look on Daniel's face I'd say I put up more of a fight then you did," she retorts while eyeing me like I'm some spineless gossip.

"Your family is crashing our breakfast but they're not welcome to dinner," I say as Lily hands her baby to Daniel and pulls out more dishes to carry into the house. I turn in time to see the stuffed duffel bag that Gloria grabs from the backseat. "Or dessert."

The tiny smirk that she shoots my way beats the embarrassed blush I expected by a mile.

"Let's eat," Gloria says nudging me towards my cabin. "And then let's kick them out."

As always, the conversation is warm and easy with Daniel and Lily. I've always welcomed their company but today is a little different. Having Gloria seated at my table with her family is like finding a piece of myself that was missing.

"Shawn, your cabin is lovely, but you need help with the interior," Lily says while side eyeing my empty bookshelves and the piles of books on the floor. It's not the first hint she's dropped, and her gentle chiding is warranted.

"Yeah, I've been slacking a bit," I admit with a wince. "It's just me here and I just got used to letting it be a little messy."

"Well Gloria is an organization queen. I'm sure she'll help you while she's in town for the weekend," Daniel says around a bite of waffle. The effort of keeping the syrup from dripping on himself or the baby taking most of his focus.

"Actually, she's extending her vacation," Lily corrects from the other side of the table. "Exploring what the mountain has to *offer* before she returns to the city."

"Is that the time?" Gloria asks glancing at a nonexistent clock on my wall and standing up. "You better get going. Don't want to keep Mama Mary waiting."

"But I'm not done!" Daniel says with half a waffle dangling from his fork.

"Eat it on the way back to your cabin," Gloria retorts with zero sympathy. "You interrupted my morning and my breakfast."

Daniel spins in his chair and makes a gesture towards Gloria like he wants me to correct her. But I'm too busy smiling over her use of my nickname for Daniel's mother to offer my help. All that comes of his effort is the waffle splashing into a syrup puddle.

"Gloria said you're done," I say with a smile. "Bye Daniel."

"I'm teaching them all the bad words!" Daniel yells over his shoulder as Lily drags him out of my cabin.

My laughter follows him out.

"I'm going to put this in the bedroom," I say while grabbing her duffel bag. It weighs more than I expected but that just means she packed enough for the week and not just the weekend.

"You don't mind?" Gloria's voice wavers behind me and I'm reminded we've never discussed our relationship. I know what I want but I haven't told her. Haven't had time with Daniel's rude ass wake up call.

I set the duffel on the bed before I answer her. The bed I made while she was gone.

"No, Sweet I don't mind at all. I want you here," I say sitting down on the edge of the bed. I fight the urge to tease and make jokes. I want to lighten the mood. Serious conversations have never been easy for me, but I know that

Gloria is worth the discomfort that comes with bearing my soul.

"I don't want you to ever leave," I whisper as she steps into the circle of my arms. "And I think you're on the same page." I add with a side glance at the bag she packed.

"I extended my vacation," she whispers back.

Her delicate hands run the width of my chest, squeezing my shoulders in her firm grip.

"I made room in the closet and the dresser," I reply.

I cleaned out half the closet and emptied dresser drawers before seeing her packed bag. The thrill that went through me at the sight can't be described. The warmth, the burst of joy, the contentment that threatens to overwhelm me is a treasure I hold close to my soul.

"Then I will stay." Her smile is bright, and it breathes life into me with its radiance. We both know that she's talking about more than the week ahead of us. It might be too much to admit right now, but we both know the truth.

A week ago, I thought this was something I would never achieve. A woman looking at me like I've made her dreams come true. A week ago, the idea of a wife and a family was a blurry dream. Now I can see it clearly.

Gloria and I living out on this mountain, supporting her work in software development, coming home from a long shift to her warm embrace. Children with eyes in shades of blue with dark hair and her little nose. Sons who can navigate with the stars and daughters who can skin a deer. Little mountaineers that are a perfect mix of us two.

I want it more than my next breath.

Gloria

This past week has been incomparable.

I worried that I was being too impulsive. That my infatuation would wither, and I would slink out of Crescent Ridge with my tail tucked between my legs. But now I'm sure of my decision.

Calling my boss with my resignation was a leap of faith and it has more than paid off. I haven't told Shawn that I made the decision yet, but he's been hinting that he doesn't want me to leave.

He keeps making more room and asking for my input about design changes. Do I want to start a vegetable garden? Should we purchase an annual subscription for that one streaming service with our favorite sitcom?

It started with trivial things like asking me to help him sort out his books. Three bookshelves later and now all his books have homes.

"Do you have a lot of books?" he asked me once I organized them by author alphabetically.

"More than you by far," I replied.

Two days later he put in an order with a friend who made all his other shelves. And that was when I called my boss. He hasn't asked me to marry him or to move in, but he's been clear where his intentions lie. Actions always speak louder than words.

"Do you want to pick out a spot for the vegetable garden?" Shawn asked on Wednesday.

"Sure," I replied. "Just know that we might get two tomatoes or two hundred and I have no control over that."

Following him out the back door I pointed to a spot close to the house. A good amount of sun with some shade from the trees.

"What about this spot?"

"Couldn't have picked a better spot if I tried," he complimented me.

I watched as he went to his truck to grab the boards he bought to build the raised planter beds we talked about. I went back inside to prepare some sandwiches for lunch, but I couldn't help glancing out the kitchen window as I worked. Every time I looked, Shawn seemed to lose a piece of clothing.

The first to fall was his jacket, light and perfect for chilly mornings. With the sun up, and the day getting warmer, it was perfectly normal for him to shed an extra layer to keep cool.

Then his blue flannel button down joined the clothing pile leaving him in a thin white T-shirt and his worn jeans. Watching a bead of sweat trickle down his neck was the last straw. The sandwiches abandoned on the table I couldn't help myself.

"Come here," I said.

Grabbing his shirt, I pulled him to me with as much force as I could manage.

"Took you long enough to bring your pretty ass back out here," Shawn grumbled before leaning down to kiss me.

"You were taunting me?"

"For the last thirty minutes at least. I've been walking around with a tape measure and a carpenter pencil measuring random things. Did you not notice the act?"

"No," I mumbled. "I was a little distracted."

"Any longer and the shirt was coming off," he says pulling the shirt over his head and tossing it on a grassy patch of soil several feet away.

"Toolbelt too?" I ask toying with the leather tie holding it up.

"You had ten minutes before I was going to walk back inside naked."

"I'd like to see that sometime."

"Noted."

I go to pull my sundress off and Shawn stops me.

"Leave it," he growls sliding his hands underneath the skirt to find my bare hips. I nod in response to his silent question.

"No panties."

"You planned this."

"To a certain extent," I admit biting my lip as he strokes a finger through my slit. "When you put on the tool belt, I made some outfit changes."

"Clever girl," he says nipping my neck as I rock my hips. Anything I can do to sink his fingers deeper. Every motion of my body brings me closer to my peak until without warning Shawn removes his fingers and leaves me on the cusp of an orgasm.

"Bastard," I groan to the sound of his laughter.

"On your back, over there in the flowers. I want those knees open wide, and I want you to start rubbing that little clit."

"Bossy."

"You love it," he says before slapping his palm against my ass.

Following his instructions, I have the skirt of my blue dress pulled up to my stomach and my pussy on display while he begins taking off his toolbelt. His cobalt eyes locked on my fingers as I stroke my core, sinking two fingers as deep as I can. They don't reach where I need them to but that's not my goal.

"Gloria," his deep rumble sends tingles down my spine as his glare meets mine.

He's not the only one who can be a tease. And it's a good time for him to learn I don't always follow orders.

His jeans and boxers are gone in a flash and before I can make a sassy comment, he's above me. Pulling my hand away from my drenched core and then his cock is pushing its way inside.

All my quips are gone as he thrusts into me. His brutal pace taking me higher and higher. My moans turn to screams as he lifts my thighs to his shoulders. Suddenly he's hitting a different angle. An angle where every thrust as me tipping closer to the edge.

"Come on my cock, Gloria," Shawn says as I writhe beneath him. "Let me feel you milk me Sweetness."

His words push me over and I'm falling into bliss. My body clenches and I feel him thrust once, twice, and then his warm seeds coats my inner walls as he fills me. Shawn catches himself before he falls onto me, rolling to his side and pulling me to lay on top of him. We're still connected as we lay in the summer sun.

Shawn

Taking Gloria into town for the summer festival was the perfect decision. As much as I want to keep her to myself, I know she needs to see what the Crescent Ridge community has to offer. Especially since her one attempt to be social ended before it began.

Introducing her to Corey and Bill as my girlfriend and parading her past the station causes my chest to swell with pride. Corey even had the gall to ask if there was a third sister. He looked crestfallen when Gloria told him no.

My cell phone ringing while we stand at a fruit display interrupts the peaceful atmosphere, but I ask Gloria to excuse me for a second when I see the name on the caller ID. The matchmaking service. After meeting Gloria, I'd meant to take my profile down, but every time I spared it a thought, she distracted me.

I try to be patient when the woman on the call tells me she has found my perfect match. The call itself is odd. Notifications of all my previous matches were delivered by email. But when she insists that this woman is an *exceptionally* good match for me, I begin to lose my temper.

"I don't care who it is," I argue with the woman. "I want to take my profile down."

The woman on the other end isn't having it. If she's to be believed she isn't just another employee, she is *the* Pearl from Pearl's Matchmaking Service. And she's trying to convince me not to ruin her successful matchmaking percentage.

"She's not your average bride," Pearl argues despite my protest. "She is assertive and direct. Not to mention that she is fully on board to move to Crescent Ridge and marry you right now."

"I'm trying to tell you," I say through gritted teeth. "I've already met my match."

"I'll just have to tell Gloria Porter the sad news then," Pearl says in a sad tone.

There is the briefest pause while she lets me process her words.

"Or maybe you could tell her yourself," she says with a mischievous lilt in her voice before hanging up on me.

I spin back around to face my girlfriend to find her kneeling on one knee with tears in her eyes and a black velvet box in her hand.

"I made a call," she says with a smile. "Shawn Langley, will you marry me?"

My words leave me as I look down at Gloria. Her curly brunette hair framing her face and her soft blue eyes peering up at me with so much hope. I don't mean to keep her waiting for an answer, but the words catch in my throat.

I try to smile even as I feel the tears running down my face.

"Yes," I finally say. "Of fucking course I'll marry you."

The grin that stretches her face before she launches herself into my arms is everything to me. I'll do anything to protect that smile.

It's not until I hear the clapping that I realize we've drawn a crowd.

"Congrats," Daniel calls out just as Lily runs forward to hug her sister.

"Thanks," I manage to say as I wipe the tears from my face. I can count on one hand the number of times I've cried. But the joy that filled my chest when I saw Gloria down on one knee just boiled over. She's one hundred percent in this for the long haul. And unlike other women she's seen the dangerous side to this way of life, and it didn't scare her off.

My city girl is becoming a mountain woman and I'm just glad she's mine.

Epilogue

Gloria

*T*wo Years Later

"Three toddlers on a hike, what could go wrong?" Shawn asks from behind me where he is carrying two of the boys. Riley, our youngest nephew is strapped to his back and our son, Sam is in another carrier on his chest. *"Everything."*

"You said it would be good practice." I say with a shrug, immediately spinning to face the trail before he can see my smirk.

The summit trailhead that we're hiking is a short trail. When it's not storming and slowing your progress that is. Or when you have three fussy children. Percy is still trudging along beside me but I suspect we'll be carrying him before too much longer. The hike up to the summit was easy going and the children were full of giggles and smiles. After some snacks and a small nap, Percy's mood took a turn for the worse.

"As my wife, it is your duty nay your obligation to prevent me from putting us into these situations."

"Lily and Daniel were due for some child free time," I remind Shawn about the circumstances that led to him volunteering us to babysit. Lily is nearing the end of her third pregnancy and chasing two children around the house daily is exhausting.

"I don't know how Mary does it," Shawn mutters as he catches up to me. "She never seems tired when we pick up Sam."

"She naps when the boys do," I say with a grin.

"How are we going to do this next year with two children?"

"We'll find a way," I say rubbing my little baby bump. "Or we'll ask Lily and Daniel to babysit."

"Five kids?" Shawn asks in a high-pitched tone. "Daniel will kill me."

"You do realize that we'll be watching five kids from time to time as well."

"*No.*"

"Yes." Enjoying the look of horror on his face and the fear I see shining in his eyes, I can't help but add a little bit more, "Not to mention when they get a bit older, they'll start having sleepovers. And when they go to school, they'll make friends, and their friends will want to come over and spend the night too. There could be six or even a dozen kids at our cabin on some nights."

"I've been tricked. Hoodwinked. Betrayed."

"Love you, Shawn."

"Love you too, Sweet."

When we finally reach the truck parked in the new gravel parking lot Shawn is quick to load the boys into their car seats while I pack away the picnic supplies.

"A dozen? Really?" he asks while we're driving back to Daniel's cabin.

"Once a year or so for birthdays. Usually, it'll just be their cousins or a close friend."

"Here I thought I married a sweet woman."

"You were wrong."

"Never been so happy to be wrong in my life. You woke me up and made me realize that my life was bland before I met you. You brought sweetness into my life and now I'll never stop craving you."

I smile at my husband as our nephews settles down in the backseat. The drive back to our cabin lulls Percy into another nap. I know when he wakes up, we'll have a cranky child on our hands again, but I wouldn't change a thing.

My life, despite all its bumps and flaws, was always meant to be here on this mountain. With this mountain man of mine we'll forge a path filled with love and laughter and that is the most beautiful thing in this world.

The End

Meet a socially awkward mountain man who accuses his mail order bride of catfishing him in Mountain Man's Rejected Mail Order Bride.

Or

Follow Jeb as he lives off grid and becomes obsessed with his own pixie stalker in Reclusive Mountain Man's Mail Order Bride.

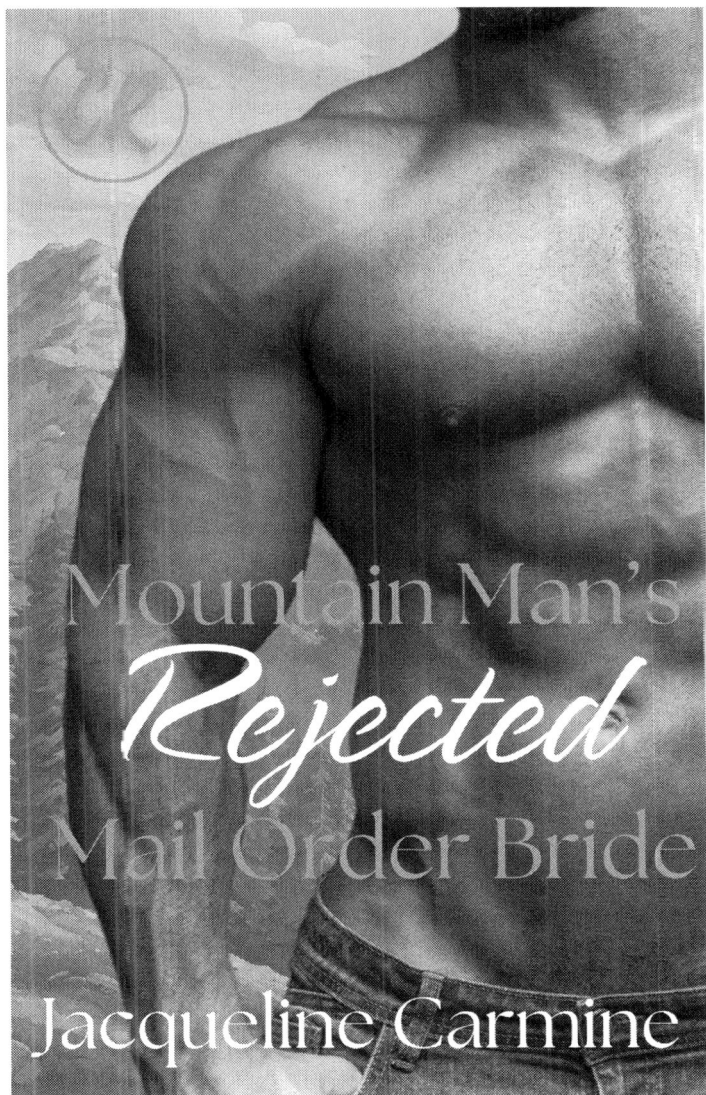

Mountain Man's
Rejected
Mail Order Bride

Jacqueline Carmine

Contents

Poppy

I'm a mail order bride. Just saying the words in my head sounds odd. Telling my coworkers and boss was an out of body experience. The club manager laughed so hard one of the girls had to fetch his inhaler. But we live in Las Vegas so it's not headlining the list of weird for any of us. We've seen outrageous things. All the tourists living by the philosophy 'What happens in Vegas, stays in Vegas' creates some rather interesting drama.

Sorry folks, that spur of the moment marriage is valid outside of Nevada. No, drugs are not legal in Vegas. The list goes on. At the end of the day agreeing to marry a near stranger didn't even crack the top ten. I've had my fair share of impulsive decisions. Stripping being one of the larger ones.

I never planned to be a stripper and in truth no one ever does. But ballet barely paid the bills and when I aged out of the troupe, I didn't have a backup plan. I always assumed I would make it big immediately and retire well off when I was ready. With only dancing on my resume, I didn't have many options and stripping paid the best.

And even if I'm dancing to club music for men's entertainment, I'm still dancing.

But my life is hardly over at thirty. I was ready for a change. When I watched girl after girl leave the club to pursue serious relationships it left a longing in my chest. Over time a new dream rose from the ashes of my failed career. I want to be a wife. I want a love so strong the man can't look anywhere but at me.

Whether my clothes are on or off.

Between the demanding schedule of ballet and then the judgement that came from stripping I had only a few serious boyfriends in my twenties.

And with little experience and no social life outside of the club I went on dating websites and found nothing worth pursuing. No one was a good enough match to justify a second date.

Until one day I found Pearl's. Her company's success rate was boastful, but I tried it on a whim. Background check passed and identity verified I started reviewing profiles within the same week.

Only one caught my eye.

A rugged mountain man smiled at me from his profile picture, and I melted into my chair. For the first time I seriously considered marrying a stranger. To have a man like that look at me like I was his entire world was everything I was chasing.

Now that I'm on the plane, moving my entire life to the mountains to be with this man, I wish I knew more about my fiancé. We've chatted through text and emails since we were matched by Pearl's Matchmaking Service.

I know from his profile that he's handsome. He has a strong jaw covered by a dark beard and heart stopping brown eyes underneath a mop of unruly brown hair. His height is listed as 6'2 and I'm a tad skeptical. Men always lie about their height on dating websites, but I'll see for myself soon enough.

Nervous energy courses through me and I struggle not to fidget in my seat. I've packed as much clothing as I could fit into my suitcase and carry on. The rest of my apartment is packed up and my friend Angie is going to supervise the movers so that I can come out to meet William sooner. He wanted to pick me up at the airport, but I told him I would meet him the day after I got into town. I need time to settle in and get the lay of the land, so I don't come off as weird.

Besides, I don't want to meet my future husband in a pair of gray sweatpants and a blue hoodie with the lettering peeling off. This outfit and my rat's nest of hair would send any man running for the hills. Or mountains in this case.

I wanted to be comfy for my trip, and comfy I am. The people around me can sit in their starched suits and scratchy denim, but I'm going to lounge without a drop of makeup on and luxuriate in the sheer relief of not giving a fuck what anyone thinks.

William

Poppy is flying in today and my nerves are wound so tight I might snap in half before her plane lands. I honestly didn't think I would match with anyone when I signed up with Pearl's. Everyone knows about Daniel's success, and I've heard all the men down at the fire station have signed up now too. But I didn't think I would find anyone that would suit me.

Seeing her face appear in my inbox floored me. The woman was drop dead gorgeous with luminous green eyes and long blonde hair styled into perfect curls. If I hadn't gone through the long application process and jumped through a dozen hoops to prove my identity, I wouldn't have believed her to be real.

Texting and chatting these last few weeks have only built up the anticipation crushing my chest. She doesn't act coy. And she says exactly what she means so that I don't have to second guess where I stand with her. She's fiercely independent and she doesn't shy away from difficult conversations.

By the time we progressed from small talk to discussing our deal breakers I was committed. Every text she sent had my heart racing. The chokehold this woman has on me is undeniable.

Poppy could have anyone she wanted but she chose a gruff mountain man. Stroking a hand down my coarse beard I wonder if she'll like it in person as much as she did in the picture. It's longer now, no longer just a shadow on my jaw.

I would've shaved my beard but in our one phone call Poppy confessed that she liked how it looked on me. Her voice sounded as sweet as sugar over the phone and when the call dropped because of the thunderstorm I could've kicked the cell tower responsible.

She didn't want to meet me at the airport but I'm not waiting another second to meet my wife. I don't have the strength to stay away, not when I know she's finally within reach.

"Today is the day huh?" Liam's voice breaks through the wind as he joins me outside the florist's shop on Main Street.

"What if she doesn't like me?" I ask before my brain can filter the words.

It comes out sounding weak and insecure, but it reveals the truth that's been circling my mind like a shark for the last three months. A woman like Poppy deserves more than a man like me can provide.

"Then you'll go your separate ways, and you'll find the woman who loves you quirks and all." His reply is quick and succinct.

Like myself he's a bit of a no-nonsense type of man. Ask him a question and you'll get a direct answer. I might have the advantage of height but thanks to his woodworking business he's got more bulk than I could ever dream of possessing. I might be tall, but I've always been thin.

"What kind of flowers do women like?" I ask.

"Varies from woman to woman," Liam replies while I scan the shop from the wide display window.

"There's so many," I reply mournfully.

"As many types of flowers as kinds of women." His tone is playful, and I know he's laughing at my expense.

"She's pretty," I admit.

"Trust me, Will, all women are pretty." His words remind me that I'm not doing a particularly good job of describing my bride.

"She's a dancer," I tell him.

It's one of the first things we talked about. Her passion for ballet and how lost she felt when her career ended.

"Not helpful," he says dismissively.

"She's nice and sweet, like a cupcake. She didn't complain about the horde of cat memes I texted her or any of my hyper fixations."

"Mrs. Clarke would probably be the person to ask for a recommendation," Liam says as he nods towards the woman arranging a bouquet of lilies behind the counter.

I know she would be helpful. And she's kind to boot. But it's hard enough asking Liam for help. He's always been the most understanding about my lack of social skills.

"Poppy deserves the best."

"Her name is Poppy?"

"I didn't tell you her name?" I ask.

It wouldn't be the first time I let a major detail slip by.

I had known Liam for several weeks before he told me we didn't share the same first name. Something that never came to my mind. It didn't click until he explained that his name can be a nickname for 'William'.

"Nope. There's your answer, buy her a bouquet of her namesake."

"Of course!" I say slapping my palm to my forehead. "But what if that's too cheesy?"

"She'll appreciate the gesture, and you can find out her favorite flower for next time."

Poppy

The Viridian Mountains are as beautiful as William promised. Towering over Bramble, Colorado and covered in frosted evergreens shape the horizon and the view is just as he described. Even on a plane miles away the majesty took my breath away. Somewhere in those mountains is the small town my future husband calls home, and I can't wait to see it.

Disembarking with the other passengers I follow the crowd as we enter a small airport. It's so tiny that it doesn't have the shops and large guideposts that were common at metropolitan airports. If I look to either side, I can see everything this airport has to offer.

Once off the plane every other passenger scattered to meet loved ones or be the first in line to rent a car or taxi. With everyone darting around it was easy to notice the hulking mountain of a man off to the side. Standing at least a head above everyone, he wears jeans and a green plaid flannel so tight I can see every bulge of muscle.

He looks like a body building god, and I'm wearing sweatpants. Even as I feel slightly put out that he ignored my request to meet later, I swallow my pride and approach him with a smile.

Eyes locking on mine I watch as the relaxed expression on his face morphs into a frown. Coming to a stop in front of him, we size each other up. His brown eyes draw me in just as I knew they would. Over the last three months, I had tried to imagine how his eyes would light up with happiness or darken with lust. Now I watched as emotion darkens his eyes.

Just not with lust.

I'm happy to see him, even dressed as I am, but I'm not a fool. He isn't happy to see me, but I can't understand why. Had he changed his mind since this morning when we last texted and confirmed my trip details?

"William?" I ask even though it's unnecessary. He looks just like his picture. No editing or filter needed when you look like you are carved from the very mountain you live on.

"You don't look like your picture," he says accusingly.

I felt a sharp pain in my stomach but ignored it.

"I don't look that different," I argue.

A little makeup could do a lot. Hide my acne and even out my skin tone. One of the new girls called me a shapeshifter. I didn't think it was that drastic, but I didn't want to make a bad first impression either.

"You totally catfished me!" he says with a sharp tone.

"Excuse me?" I ask with a tone to match.

Sharp not shrill. God save the man if he calls me a screeching harpy like my ex.

"You're not even blonde!" he yells.

It takes every bit of will in my body not to lash out physically. I doubt I would be able to do any considerable damage anyway, but I wanted to try. So, help me. I want to kick the bastard's shins.

I'm tired of touching up my roots every few weeks. I thought moving to a quiet mountain town I would be able to let go of the constant maintenance on my hair.

"It's called hair dye jackass," I say resisting the urge to stomp my foot.

I wasn't going to tell him this was my natural color. Or close enough that when the roots grew out again, they would be a close match. A pang of guilt stabbed at my conscience. I was so eager and wrapped up in the process of moving I didn't tell him I wasn't a natural blonde.

"And your eyes aren't green," he adds in a mild voice.

Okay maybe that one was a fair criticism. And the fact that he wasn't yelling anymore helped to cool my ire.

"Colored contacts," I murmur in acknowledgment.

Maybe I had misrepresented myself. Just a bit. Back in the city everyone put on so many layers to hide their flaws and make themselves feel better. A bit like wearing a mask so that you can pretend to be someone else. Someone more confident or more secure.

And I always got better tips as a blonde.

"You look too different." William's voice is a low rumble.

So low I almost didn't hear the words.

"Sorry for wasting your time," I mumble, feeling like a scorned puppy.

I don't make it two steps back towards the ticket counter before the embarrassment heating my cheeks twists into bitter anger. Spinning around sharply I stare down the mountain man I came all this way to marry.

"No, I'm not sorry. You're a jackass and I wish I never matched with you. You're just like every other man on the strip. All you care about is how I look. Never mind that I came all this way, cancelled my lease, and packed up my entire life to take a chance on the likes of you!"

His brown eyes are wide, and I watch as his mouth moves without sound.

Perfect.

"The only thing I'm sorry about is that you are clearly not the man I thought you were."

With those parting words I leave him in my dust as I head to the car rental counter. Screw him. I'm not getting back on the plane two seconds after arriving. I already arranged the car rental, and my hotel room is booked. I just need to grab the keys, and I will turn this trainwreck into something positive.

The wedding might be off, but I can still have a vacation while I'm in town. Take in the mountain views, do a little shopping, or even go on a hike. Something to take my mind off all the arrangements I need to make. I need to call my landlord ASAP. Not to mention the moving company and my old boss.

That man is going to laugh himself into another asthma attack when I do call and beg for my job back. If I bother. My life is already packed up and maybe Bramble will need a ballet instructor. Even without the man I can still get the mountain.

William

I watch as Poppy walks away from me. I feel the stares
stabbing at me as I stand frozen watching the woman
I want as my wife walk away. She is beautiful. So far out of
my league I might as well be a mole in the dirt beneath her
feet. She was pretty in the photo but seeing her in person
was like trying to talk with all the air sucked out of my
chest.

It all went wrong. Horribly wrong. Every word out of
my mouth was wrong. She looked so happy stepping off
the plane and her eyes lit up when she saw me waiting for
her at the gate. And then I opened my mouth and a whole
lot of stupid came out.

Glancing at the red bouquet of poppies in my hand I
make a snap decision. I could let my anxiety rule me or I

could go after the woman who made me feel like my heart beats for her alone.

She has a head start but the line for car rentals is long.

"Excuse me. There's a line in case you didn't notice," a man in a three-piece suit says as I approach Poppy.

"Poppy," I say to get her attention.

She doesn't acknowledge me. She doesn't even pretend not to hear me. Her huff of breath is louder than the chatter surrounding us.

"Sir! There is a line," the man standing behind Poppy says again.

"I'm not cutting. I'm here to retrieve my wife." I say to the man over my shoulder.

He looks miffed but doesn't bother me again as I try to think of a way to dig my way out of this hole. The words I need desperately won't come and my addled brain leaves me standing like an ominous shadow beside the petite brunette.

"Are you just going to stand there all day?" Poppy's words were direct and loud.

"If I need to I will," I say to her.

"I'm not some *thing* to be retrieved," she says while giving me a stern look. "And I am not your wife."

"Yet," I add.

"Never gonna happen." Her words sound sure, but her foot is tapping against the tile. That nervous tick gives me the courage to keep talking. To find the words.

"I panicked," I say as the line slowly moved forward as a person got assigned a car. "I was caught off guard and I didn't tell you any of the things I wanted to say."

"It's not what you didn't say. It's what you *did* say," she says while yet another person is given a set of keys.

"Agreed. I tend to put my foot in my mouth. You're not what I expected." The excuse sounds lame even to my ears, but I have a limited time to explain my quirks.

"I was dressed to the nines in the picture I sent you. It didn't take a smart man to realize I wouldn't look that good all the time."

"You're beautiful," I tell her honestly.

She isn't the blonde with green eyes I expected to step off the plane, she's better. I'm dying to touch her hair and see if it's as soft as it looks. The soft scent of lilacs and vanilla carries on an air-conditioned breeze.

"My face is breaking out and my hair is a mess. And you weren't supposed to see me in *these,*" she says as she pinches and jerks the leg of her sweatpants between her fingers. "Until we were married at least a month."

"They look soft," I compliment her. "Most of my clothing is flannel or cotton because I like how it feels against my skin."

"They are," she says. I can see her visibly swallow as she adds, "It was a long flight, and I wanted to be comfortable."

Finally, her eyes meet mine fully and I can see the vulnerability shining within. The same tender, cautious hope that's been building in my chest since we were matched.

A long moment passes as I stare into her deep cerulean eyes. Around us people still chatted and laughed but it all sounded muffled to my ears. Even as I gaze at Poppy letting her see my own fragile sense of longing, I knew the clock was ticking down. It was almost her turn, and I was running out of time.

"I need a second chance. I can't pretend to deserve it, but I will make sure you never regret it. I will never speak to you like that again."

Her head tilts to the side and I can almost hear the wheels in her head spinning as she considers my apology.

"Before the phone call cut out during that storm you didn't say much."

"I have a hard time talking to new people."

"And yet you wanted a mail order bride."

"Sounds kind of crazy," I admit rubbing the back of my head.

I go to stick my other hand in the pocket of my denim jeans and stop just in time to avoid crushing the flowers I'm still holding.

"These are for you," I say as I hold them out for Poppy's inspection.

"Thank you," she says taking them from me and giving them an admiring look. The same look she had blessed me with before I opened my mouth and ruined it.

"Next!" calls the car rental employee and I watch Poppy's face as she looks from the counter to me. I didn't breathe until she turned to the man behind us and told him to go ahead.

The crushing weight on my chest lifts as she turns to me without any trace of irritation or anger on her face. She's giving me a second chance. And I'm not going to fuck it up.

I take her bag from her as she loops her arm around mine. I match my longer strides to her shorter ones as I lead her to my truck so that she doesn't have to run to keep up with me.

"What did you want to tell me?" She must have seen my confusion because she quickly added, "You said you didn't say any of the things you wanted to when we met."

I pause for only a moment before the speech I had planned comes pouring out of me. I spent hours choosing the right words while she was booking her flight and arranging her move.

"I know you lost your dream when you left ballet. But I'm so happy that you found a new one and that it led you to me. I'll do everything in my power to make every one of your dreams come true, because you're my dream."

"That's too fucking sweet," she says as she wipes away the tears running down her face.

"I'm not good with people or words. I speak bluntly before my brain catches up. I stare too long and often. People say I'm hard to read," I say as I reach across to buckle her seat belt.

"I was a stripper," she says as I climb into the cab.

"You dropped a lot of hints. Enough for even me to catch on."

"You don't care?" she asks with her voice just a hair above a whisper.

"No. You said you would marry me. That you would teach dance classes in town," I tell her.

Her life before we met isn't going to influence our relationship. She found a job and paid her bills until she found me. The details don't matter in the grand scheme of things. Maybe other men would be bothered but they're fools. Poppy couldn't find a man worth her time in Vegas and their loss is my gain.

"Just like that?"

"Just like that. Although if you ever wanted to give me a private dance I wouldn't complain," I say with a wink and a cheeky grin.

"On your birthday, maybe," she replies with a matching grin.

"Now, are we going to the courthouse or to my cabin?"

"I'm not marrying you in sweatpants," Poppy fires back with a smile bright enough to blind me.

Poppy

The judge didn't finish declaring us married before William's mouth covered mine. His lips were warm and soft against mine. His wiry beard brushing my cheeks and chin as he kissed me like his life depended on it.

"Save it for the honeymoon!" The judge chastised us when our kiss didn't end after an appropriate amount of time.

"Sorry," William apologizes to the judge when we separate. His cheeks are as red above his beard as mine feel.

Making the short trip to the hotel room was worth it. I twirl out the courthouse doors letting my white sundress flair out. The heat hasn't left William's eyes since we got to the hotel. Keeping my hands off him has become progressively more difficult. It's not a religious choice but I've gone thirty years without sex. It didn't seem like a challenge to wait a few more hours until we were officially married.

I know my first time isn't going to be a magical moment but something about the idea of my first time being with my husband strikes a chord in my heart.

"I know we agreed not to have a traditional wedding, but I would like to stop by the bakery and get us a cake."

"I'll never say no to good food," William says in a warm rumble. "There is one bakery in town, and you'll love it. And Mrs. Carmichael, she's warm and friendly and everything she bakes melts in your mouth."

"I can't wait to meet her."

William takes my hand and holds it the entire way to the bakery. The air is warm, and the wind kicks up cooling my heated cheeks. Everything about the town of Crescent Ridge feels like a dream. Red brick buildings with cobblestone streets and small mom and pop shops without a chain store in sight. People wave as we pass and William knows everyone, telling me names and tidbits as we go. It's a far cry from the neon eccentricity that is Vegas.

It's as perfect as he promised.

We enter the bakery aptly named *Sugar Crossing* and the smell of freshly baked cookies hits me like a slap in the face.

"William darling, is this your new bride?" a woman with a round face calls out behind the counter.

Her grey hair tied back in a neat bun with a few tendrils loose to frame her face. I know without asking that this is

Mrs. Carmichael. Even if she wasn't the only one working, her brown eyes are warm and shine with kindness.

"Yes, this is Poppy," William says, leading me forward with a warm hand pressing against my bare back. I try not to be distracted by the tingles his touch elicits from my body.

"What a beautiful bride you make my dear," Mrs. Carmichael says with a gentle smile, the corners of her lips tilting up slightly.

"Thank you. I heard you make the best cakes."

"I do indeed." She grabs a white box from underneath the counter. "Caramel apple coffee cake is a bestseller but it's not decadent enough for a wedding. What about a rich triple chocolate cake?"

"Sounds delicious," I say.

Honestly when is there ever a bad time for chocolate? I look up at William to see him grinning from ear to ear.

"Some of my cakes are fancier but it's always the old simple recipes that keep customers coming back."

William

Getting my wife home to our cabin takes longer than I expected. Always a bit left footed with social interactions. I didn't anticipate the warm welcome from the other locals. The waving on our way to buy our wedding cake was expected but I didn't think anyone would seek us out. Liam was the first, going out of his way to find us at the bakery.

"Poppy!" His voice booms as he enters the small eatery. "Finally, we meet."

Poppy's smile is warm but when she goes for a handshake he pulls her into a hug, lifting her off her feet. Her squeak of surprise is the only sign that he caught her off guard. With a laugh she hugs him back.

"You must be Liam! William speaks highly of you," Poppy says as Liam sets her back onto her feet.

Trying to curb the sharp stab of jealousy that formed when he took *my* wife into his arms, I wrap an arm around Poppy's shoulders drawing her to my side.

"Liam, what a surprise. I thought you'd be at work."

"And miss the opportunity to meet your wife? Not a chance."

"We were about to head home," I say before Poppy can begin fawning over the bulky man again.

"Bring her by the workshop sometime and I'll get those measurements for that rocking chair," Liam says before abandoning us for Elaine Carmichael's bear claws.

The irony of a man built like a bear eating them isn't lost on anyone. Not even me.

"He's just as nice as you said," Poppy says as we exit the bakery and return to my truck.

I bite back a growl but just barely.

"Oh stop. He was just being friendly," she admonishes me, clearly reading my jealousy as easily as she breathes.

"Too friendly," I mutter as I reach over to buckle her in.

I like that she doesn't question the action. I know others consider my quirks to be odd or weird. To have her just *accept* my actions as normal is something I didn't dare dream.

"You're just grumpy," she says with the same warm smile she's worn since we said our vows.

I'm overwhelmed for a moment as I remember that this delicate woman is *mine*. That I'm her husband. Despite the rocky start we're a family.

"Liam is a good man." I say around the lump in my throat. "I'm just jealous that he got to hold you before I did."

"Well, considering that you're going to be the one holding me *all night long*. I think we can give the man a pass," she replies quick as a whip, and I find myself caught between the urge to laugh or hide my face.

I haven't told her that I'm a virgin.

I was teased through high school for my social awkwardness, and Liam is the only person I've ever told. He's been a good friend to me all these years. I cringe as I think of the way I dismissed him after he went to the effort to meet my wife. Especially after he helped me with my panic over the flowers.

Flowers that Poppy keeps sniffing and admiring as we drive up the mountain.

It's not often that Liam needs my help. Working in computer programming is great for working remotely without the need for human interaction. It makes good money but it's not a life skill I can transfer into the physical world. Still, I will find a way to return his kindness. Maybe help him set his business up online or something similar.

"Did you grow up here?" Poppy's question catches me off guard and I look over to see an indulgent look on her face.

"Sorry. I tend to get lost in my head from time to time," I explain with a wince. It drove my mother mad when I was growing up. "I grew up in Denver. But I never liked being around people and once I got my degree, I found a job working remotely. After that I searched for a place where I could be far away from people but still have internet."

"You picked a beautiful town," she says.

I hope she'll like our home as much as she likes Crescent Ridge. I know from experience that mountain life is drastically different from the conveniences of the city.

"Our cabin isn't anything grand, but it is more modern than how some of the other men live on this mountain. Or so I'm told."

"You only mentioned Liam while we were chatting. Do you have any family nearby? A mother who is going to be jealous I'm married to her favorite son?"

"Only child and my mother visits once a year."

"Isn't she going to be mad she wasn't invited to our wedding?"

"No," I tell Poppy. I would like to leave it as simple as that, but I can see the curiosity on her face. As my wife, she deserves to know. "She visits out of obligation. She blames me for my father's death."

I see Poppy's eyes widen and I know I'll have to tell her the entire tale, but I don't want to do that today. This is our wedding day, and I want it to be perfect. It'll do no good to dwell on ghosts of the past. And I tell her as much.

"Okay, but full story tomorrow. I'm not letting you off the hook."

"I would expect nothing less."

Poppy

The drive up to the cabin is gorgeous. We follow a winding road cutting a path through a forest of pine trees with the occasional curve showing the steep drop off the side. We pass several gravel drives leading deep into the trees without any sign of houses visible. My ears pop with the increase in elevation.

"This is us," William says before entering a paved driveway.

I didn't ask about his house. Finding out more about my potential husband seemed so much more important than asking how big his house was or if it had crown molding.

Please no crown molding.

As we pull up to the house I'm blown away by the sheer size. I knew it would be bigger than my studio apartment. Such a tiny, crammed space how could any house be smaller? But William's house? It doesn't belong in the mountains.

It has a wooden framing in a light varnish with massive glass windows. From the outside I can see a large sectional and a fireplace in the living room. Terracotta steps lead up to a large black door with silver handles. He has flower beds planted on each side of the porch steps filled with plants in full bloom. Red, yellow, blue, and purple flowers fill the beds to bursting.

"Magnificent," I say in a whisper.

"I'm glad you like it," William says with a grin. "I know it's not exactly mountain chic, but it is home."

"I think I expected some sort of log cabin," I say as he leads me up the front steps.

"Some of the other men have cabins like those," William says. "And Jeb actually has one without electricity or plumbing."

I didn't marry William for his house, but I'm more than a little grateful he has modern conveniences. I could live in a house much smaller, but I can't imagine the kind of woman who could live without indoor plumbing in this day and age.

"I hired an architect, interior designer, and a landscape artist when I bought this land," William says as he shows me the house. "There are very few materialistic things I'm emotionally attached to, so we can change paint colors and hardware to whatever you like."

Looking around the house I can tell it lacks a certain warmth, like a human touch. But it is beautiful and comforting all the same. And I tell my husband as much.

"What are you attached to?" I ask when he shows me the bedrooms on the second floor.

"My work area and my bed," William replies without missing a beat.

When he shows me our bedroom I almost squeal at the size of the bed. I've heard of sizes bigger than a king, but I didn't consider exactly how much bigger they can get.

"Alaskan King, it's like sleeping on a cloud," William says when he sees me drooling over the bed. "And I collect soft pillows."

Dozens of throw pillows cover the bed. Some are made of satin and others faux fur, some in neutral tones and some in vibrant hues. The bed is an odd eclectic mix of patterns and styles.

I love it.

"And this is where I work," William says waving a hand at the large desk overlooking a wide window with a view of the mountain side.

On his desk he has three large monitors with a fourth mounted to the wall above it. His computer chair is black with silver accents and the entire set up is situated on a faux fur rug in grey. He must take my silence as a negative reaction because he rubs the back of his neck while a red blush tints his cheeks.

"I like to be comfortable," he says in explanation.

"I like the room, William," I tell him with a smile. "Las Vegas was a wild place to live but it was home. And it was a crazy mix of neon, sequins and fur. Our bedroom reminds me of it just a little bit, and that makes it feel like home."

His eyes darken when I refer to the bedroom as ours. The passion in his eyes is empowering. He's seen me at my worst, with my acne flaring up and without a touch of makeup on my face and still he looks at me like I'm the most delectable thing he's ever seen.

"Would you like to have dinner now or later?" William asks and his question catches me off guard.

We just got married and we're in our bedroom. I'll be damned if the honeymoon doesn't start right now.

"No," I say walking up to him. I stroke my hand down his chest in my best seductive manner while looking at him from under my eyelashes. "I'd rather have dessert."

"There is cake downstairs," William replies, the heat in his eyes is the only hint that he's teasing me.

"I was thinking something more creamy," I purr.

"We have ice cream in the freezer," William says with a chuckle.

"Is it organic? Locally sourced?" I ask. Before he can reply I shake my head and add, "Because I like my cream straight from the source."

My hand brushing against his cock through his pants illustrates my point. Even as we both burst into laughter.

"I'm sorry! I shouldn't laugh," William shouts.

"No, you definitely should!" I reply wiping away the tears that came from laughing so hard. "It was definitely cringey."

"I've never done this before," William confides after we catch our breath.

"Sex?" I ask just to clarify.

"Yes."

A wave of possessiveness washes over me as I realize I will be the only woman to ride his cock. That we'll be each other's first and last. The feeling is as overwhelming as it is unexpected, and it shocks me into silence.

A silence that wipes the smile from William's mouth and I rush to make sure that he doesn't think I'm rejecting him.

I step into his space, placing my hands on his chest, and tilting my head back to look at him.

"Let's make it worth the wait then."

William

M y bride is on her knees unbuckling my pants before I realize her intent.

"If you touch me, I'll explode," I tell her as she lowers my zipper.

The stiff line of my cock tents my blue plaid boxers. Although I'm eager to have Poppy's hands on me I can't stop the rush of embarrassment at being exposed to my wife for the first time.

"Explode," Poppy says looking up at me from under-neath her dark lashes. Her wide blue eyes look up at me with so much trust I find myself falling for her just a little more.

No one has ever looked at me like that.

Like I'm the focus of her entire world. Like she loves me.

She slides my boxers down, exposing my cock to the chilled room. My pants and boxers settle around my thighs and Poppy holds my gaze as she flicks her tongue out to taste me.

"Salty," she says with a shy smile.

The blush on her cheeks gets a little brighter as suspicion begins to form in my mind. The way she fumbled with my belt buckle. Her cringey attempt at seduction with words that could've come straight from a poorly written porn script.

My thoughts melt away as her mouth wraps around the mushroom shaped tip of my cock. The warmth and gentle suction threaten to bring me to my knees. Her dark head bobs as she takes most of my length, easing back as she chokes when I hit the back of her throat. She swallows around my cock, sucking me deeper into the warm heat of her mouth.

She pulls back allowing her teeth to lightly graze the sensitive flesh as she goes.

"Tell me what you like," she says after she releases my cock with a soft popping sound.

"Everything you're doing," I grunt, not recognizing my own voice. "It all feels so good, Poppy."

She takes my length back into her mouth wrapping one hand around my base. I lose myself to the feeling of her warm mouth, bucking my hips in time with her bobbing head. Her other hand raises to my hip and her nails bite into my skin as she urges me closer.

"P-Poppy," I stutter trying to warn her as my spine tingles with my impending release. "I'm going to come, honey."

Her pace increases and I close my eyes tilting my head back as I come. My seed leaves my cock in a long spurt and Poppy takes it all, swallowing every drop. She licks her lips before swiping the heel of her palm across her mouth to wipe away any stray moisture.

As she looks up at me her cheeks darken once more, the bold vixen fading into the shy bride once more.

Disregarding the looming awkwardness of having my pants still wrapped around my thighs I hold out my hand to help her up. When she stands, I see that her knees are rubbed raw and bright red.

"Next time you'll get a pillow," I say with shame burning the back of my neck. "Or we can pick out a very plush rug, so your knees don't get hurt."

Poppy

My panties were damp at the courthouse, and they've slowly become drenched as I sucked William's cock. A large part of me was worried I would mess it up and ruin our first night together as husband and wife.

Listening to him moan as I worked his cock first with my mouth alone and then with a helping hand was a huge boost to my ego. He didn't last long with my mouth on him, helping me feel confident and empowered.

William pulls me into his embrace, pressing a languid kiss on my lips that seems to never end. His calloused fingers slip the delicate straps of my sundress off my shoulders, leaving my collarbone bare for his mouth's exploration.

His tongue and lips dance across my collarbone leaving a trail of fire burning in their wake. My nipples harden when his warm breath hits the sensitive skin of my neck and goosebumps raise on my skin.

"I couldn't dream of a better wife," he mumbles into my neck. "You knock me on my ear with a single glance."

"I'd rather knock you on your back," I whisper into his ear as I pull him towards the bed.

A firm tug on his arms has us spinning until he falls back against the bed, and I can climb onto his lap. I pull my sundress over my head allowing my breasts to swing freely as I straddle his thighs. His shirt joins my dress on the floor and suddenly my husband is completely naked.

Marveling at the muscles that the flannel did a poor job of masking I nearly catch myself melting. The skin is firm and warm beneath my fingers as he lets me explore. His thighs are covered in a light coating of dark hair that feels silky smooth against my own legs.

With his pants and boxers dropped to the floor there is only one barrier still separating us. The tiny scrap of fabric between my thighs doesn't last long.

William reaches between us snagging the thin strap around my waist with his finger and he rips it before I can protest. The white satin is tossed aside as I settle over my husband's cock for the first time.

It's thick and long enough to make me nervous but I know William will be careful. He's hard again, and it glides easily through my slick folds.

"I've never had sex before," I tell him as he grips his cock preparing to enter me for the first time.

His eyes widen and he freezes as my words hit him. I should have mentioned it before but now I can't take the words back. A moment passes as our eyes lock on each other. I see the shock in his eyes, and I watch as it fades back into that familiar warmth I'm quickly becoming accustomed to.

"I'm honored," he says relaxing beneath me. "Unbelievably fucking lucky and honored to be your first."

I begin to slide down his cock, pausing briefly as I go to allow my body to stretch around his girth.

"And last," he says his tone a growl as I sink down the last few inches until my hips meet his.

"First and last," I agree with a nod.

I rest my palms on his chest as I rock my hips back and forth slowly. His cock slides against my walls, the movement building a fire low in my belly. William's brown eyes are feral as he watches me move above him. I can feel him tensing beneath me, struggling not to rush this as he lets me set the pace.

It's only after I try to go faster, seeking my climax desperately that he breaks. His calloused hands come up to grip my hips, helping lift me up before slamming me down to meet his thrusts.

Our pace becomes frantic, our hands clutching desperately at each other as the heat builds. When I falter, pleasure leaving me boneless as my walls milk his cock, William takes my weight fully lifting me up as he thrusts into me from below.

"P-Poppy," he says as his eyes lock on mine. "I'm about to come."

"Don't pull out," I say quickly. "I want to feel all of you."

He stills beneath me, his muscles clenching as he comes, his warm seed filling me to the brim. He lowers me gently to his chest and wraps his arms around me pulling me close. We lay there in a contented pile until I fall asleep. His cock still inside me.

William

I leave my sleeping wife in our bed when the sky is still dark. She grumbles in her sleep as I slip out of the bed and put on a pair of sleeping pants. I want nothing more than to crawl back into the bed and wake her with my mouth between her legs.

But she needs to eat.

We woke up twice during the night to make love, each time starting slow with soft kisses before need turned us feral. After the second time we laid in bed, and I told her about my father's death. How he was running late to pick me up from soccer practice when he ran a red light and another car hit him.

I know it's not my fault, but my mother can't make that connection. The pain and grief have swallowed her whole.

Poppy held me close as I told her about the funeral and the difficult years that followed. My mother's way of coping was drinking and when she drank, she didn't mince her words. She told me unequivocally that it was my fault my father died. It didn't surprise anyone when I moved away as soon as I could.

In turn Poppy told me about how her parents turned their backs on her for stripping. How ashamed they were to have her as a daughter. We talked for hours before we drifted off to sleep again.

My new mission in life is to make sure that Poppy knows I'm proud of her. Proud of her past and how she took care of herself. Proud of the woman she has become without her family's support. And proud to have her as my wife and one day the mother of my children.

Looking back at my wife I feel my cock lift to half-mast despite our lovemaking just hours ago. I'd love to stay in bed and lick my wife's pussy as the sun rises. I had a brief taste between rounds two and three but not enough to sate my hunger. But if I give in that will lead to round four and she needs food before then.

I'm just putting butter on the toast when Poppy wanders down to the kitchen. She's wearing one of my old shirts, a grey one with faded lettering that hangs down to her knees. Her hair is messy, and her eyes are heavy with sleep.

She perks up with a smile that reaches her eyes when she sees the breakfast I made. The sun is rising, an orange and pink glow lighting the sky between the trees, and it casts a warm glow onto her skin.

"Is that bacon?" she asks walking over to hug me from behind while I finish plating our food.

"Locally sourced," I reply with a smirk and her tinkling laughter is my reward.

We settle at the kitchen table side by side facing the window and watch the sun rise in silence as we eat our first breakfast as husband and wife.

"What's the plan for today?" she asks while sipping from a glass of orange juice.

Her voice is light and carefree while my own is more of a grumble. My coffee warms my soul one drink at a time. Right now, I'm at a half charge despite being on my second cup for the day.

"No plan," I say with a wince.

We could go for a hike, or I could take her to town to explore.

"You don't need to work?" Her question pulls me from my thoughts.

Her smile is wide, and she seems happy that I'll be around.

"I'm taking a week off," I reply happy that I thought ahead.

"For our honeymoon?" she asks and I can't hide a grimace.

"I didn't plan any kind of trip."

I should have booked an actual honeymoon trip for my wife. Taken her someplace nice with a white sandy beach and lots of sun. And I could have watched her walk around in a tiny bikini with all her gorgeous skin on display. Sometimes I could kick my own ass.

"Don't need to leave to have a honeymoon," she says putting her glass down on the oak table.

She slides onto my lap while my brain tries to catch up. Her bare thighs spread around my waist causing the hem of her shirt to ride up.

Poppy's smirk turns my thoughts dirty in a blink. Her shirt sails through the air as I stand up to lay her on the kitchen table. She giggles at my eagerness until I wrap my lips around one of her nipples, licking the stiff peak. Her laughter fades into a moan, low and sultry.

"Never stop," she says as she arches her back.

"Never," I agree dragging my lips across her chest to the other breast.

My cock is tenting my pajama pants, the only barrier between us.

"I need you," Poppy cries as I gently scrape my teeth over her pebbled flesh.

Her hands clutch my hair twisting the strands around her fingers as she lifts her hips off the table to press herself against me. As she grinds her pussy against my cock I mutter a curse.

I wanted to take her slowly just once. Every time we've had sex has been fast and fevered. But her pleas do not go ignored. I pull at the drawstring of my pants letting them slip down my legs to pool at my feet. The head of my cock slides through her wet slit, coating it in her arousal.

I lean forward to hover over my wife, my cock sliding home easily as she releases my hair to grab my shoulders.

Her nails bite into my skin as I thrust into her. The slight pain grounds me to the moment. Seeing her face overcome with pleasure I bite the inside of my cheek to keep from coming immediately.

"You look so good taking my cock," I tell her as she writhes beneath me. "Your pussy was made for this cock."

My words cause her to tense, her body arching into mine as she grips me tightly. Her walls milk my cock as she falls apart in my arms, thrashing and clawing at me as her orgasm takes her over the edge. My hips falter as the base of my spine tingles and I come.

We rest, sweaty and sticky on the table as birds chirp in the nearby pine trees. Once we catch our breath, I help Poppy off the table, and we dress in companionable silence.

"How about a hike?" Poppy asks once she slips back into my shirt.

I look at her standing in front of the window. Hair mussed from sleep and sex, eyes bright with joy and a contented smile as she looks at me. Without thinking I say exactly what has been running through my head since the moment I saw my wife standing at that airport terminal.

"I love you," I say with my heart beating steadily in my chest. "My heart beats for you, Poppy. I don't know how I survived until now, but I never want to go back to what I was before I met you."

I don't need her to say it back. It's enough that she knows how strongly I care for her. More than anyone else I know the weight every word carries. I might not always be able to verbally express myself in the moment when I'm too overwhelmed, but I've had time to fall in love with my wife. And I know how important it is that she knows exactly what she means to me. I need her like my computer's CPU needs a fan. Like a river needs rain. I just bumbled my way through life until we matched, and now there is no going back to what life was before. Poppy and I belong together.

"William," Poppy says as her bright blue eyes shine with tears. "I love you too."

Epilogue

Poppy

Six Months Later

Leaving the ridge always leaves me feeling a bit bereft. Our home always fills me with peace and comfort and wherever we go no place feels the same. Sometimes it makes me laugh at how fast I became a homebody. I leave the house to visit friends and teach ballet in my dance studio in Crescent Ridge. But home is where the heart is and every day I spend with William only deepens our connection and our love for each other.

"Poppy!" my friend Angie calls as she exits the boarding area.

Her blonde hair is in a no-nonsense ponytail and her face is free of make-up. Her oversized sweatshirt hangs loose on her petite frame and the black yoga pants underneath only visible beneath her knees.

"Angie!" I call back, rushing to my friend.

We embrace in a tight hug as her luggage tips over clattering onto the tiled floor with a loud clack.

"The famous Angie," William says when we finally part. "Pleased to meet you."

My friend ignores his outstretched hand and steps forward to hug my husband.

"Strangers shake hands, family hugs," she says in explanation as she steps back.

William takes her behavior in stride. I did warn him in advance that she was a touchy-feely sort, just like Liam. He grabs her suitcase despite her protests and leads us through the airport.

"I can't believe I'm finally here," she says as she follows us to the truck. "And you're married!"

"Happily married," I say waving my left hand. "Maybe you'll find yourself a husband while you're here."

"Unlikely," Angie says with a small huff. "Marriage is not for me."

William and I share a look as we drive towards Crescent Ridge. Maybe we're biased because of our own love story, but I can't help feeling that the mountains will work their magic for my friend.

The men of Crescent Ridge are built different, and my gut is saying that Angie will find her very own mountain man.

The End

Meet the erotic audio content creator who changes Angie's mind in Mountain Man's Dirty Mail Order Bride.

Mountain Man's

Dirty

Nailo Maride

Jacqueline Carmine

Contents

Eric

"You haven't earned my cock yet," I breathe into the microphone. "Get on your knees and show me how badly you want me to fuck that pussy."

I can add sound effects later, but I try to get my voice as close to the desired goal as possible. I might not be the best at talking with real women, but I can talk dirty to a microphone all day.

"That's a good girl," I say with a growl. "Your bratty mouth looks so good when it's stuffed with my cock."

I click pause on my audio recording and replay the last few minutes. Everything sounds good so I continue to work on the project. I'm one of the top content creators for *Wicked Audio,* an erotic audio platform that caters to women. Women who love the sound of my voice.

By all accounts I should be a hit with the ladies. But every time I try to start up a conversation with an attractive woman, my tongue seems to tie itself in knots. I trip and stumble over my words until it doesn't matter that I'm objectively handsome with a deep sonorous voice. I'm just the bumbling fool who can't carry on the simplest conversation.

8?

The text lights up my phone and since I'm between clips I reply in the affirmative. Liam has been using my home gym for over a year now. He's a good friend who doesn't give me shit about my trainwreck record with women. So, I let him use my weights. And vent his relationship woes as he does.

Some weeks Liam's visits are the only social interaction I have. William and Liam are two of my closest friends. Liam introduced us after William moved to Crescent Ridge. The other man is socially awkward as well but his issues stem from missing social cues rather than stumbling over his words.

I go back to my audio, recording the last few lines before I shut down my studio for the night.

"I didn't say you could come on my cock," I snarl. "Stop whining. Put this cock inside your mouth and suck it clean."

By the time Liam arrives I've already got a pretty good workout in with the weights, but I still hit the treadmill for some light cardio. I sit at my desk for hours every day and if I didn't get my ass up and moving my health would be wrecked. My dad died from a heart attack at forty. I'm going to do everything in my power to ensure the same doesn't happen to me. I'm thirty and in the best shape of my life.

With guys like Liam and William pushing me to be my best I'm not worried about leaving this world the same way my dad did.

"William's wife is perfect for him," Liam says after a while.

We share a look across the room while he wipes his sweat with a white towel. I know William signed up for Pearl's Matchmaking. All three of us have but William is the only one who matched right away.

"Love at first sight?" I ask bumping up the incline.

"Yes," Liam says frowning at the treadmill. "He put his foot in his mouth in classic William fashion calling her out for catfishing him."

My eyebrows rise but I'm not surprised that William fumbled at the starting line. Not everyone handles William's blunt, tactless manner well.

"And she still married him?"

"Almost immediately after," Liam says while I pump my arms powering through the last quarter mile of my run. "And now one of her friends from Vegas is coming out to visit."

"Let me guess," I begin as I grab my own towel. "William wants to parade the eligible bachelors out in a bid to convince her to move out here."

"Happy wife, happy life," Liam replies, raising his water bottle up in a salute.

Angie

Crescent Ridge might be just another small town in the mountains, but it has the most gorgeous sights I've ever seen. Five minutes downtown and I've already seen twenty tanned, toned, and handsome men. Each seems to tower above the last and after a moment the faces begin to blur. All I see are shirts clinging to large frames threatening to rip at the seams.

Poppy and William are taking me to the local fire station to introduce me to some of the locals including Liam. He's one of William's best friends and Poppy has dropped a dozen hints that we would make a fantastic couple.

One minute in his company and I can confirm that Poppy is nuts.

He's hot, don't get it twisted. Blonde and barrel chested with the Fire and Rescue logo stamped over his black

T-shirt that is straining against his pecs, a woman would be crazy not to find him attractive. He's a volunteer firefighter and he's made a career out of woodworking. Heroic and an entrepreneur.

Liam will make one woman a wonderful husband.

Just not me.

I want a man with a sultry voice that makes my toes curl even when he's reading a grocery list. Ever since my last relationship went up in flames, I've turned to audio erotica while masturbating. A man growling low in my ear as he praises me or a degrading laugh that causes tingles to race up my spine never fails to turn me on.

Especially *LingeringFev3r,* the one creator I keep coming back to over and over again. The way he moans low and long when he orders me to suck his cock never fails to send me soaring over the edge of ecstasy.

Logically I know that he's not talking to *me.* And no man can measure up to a voice that is edited with special effects. He's a voice actor and nothing more.

But I want a man who can talk me to orgasm. And Liam's not that man. He's warm and polite, even if his smile doesn't reach his eyes. But his voice doesn't make me want to drop my panties and ride his dick. I won't be dating William's best friend and going on double dates with Poppy anytime soon. Judging by her pinched eyebrows she's realized we're not hitting it off.

"Liam," A deep voice says from behind me.

In a flash my panties are damp. The rumbling baritone is one I've listened to more nights than not. Against all odds, the man who inspires all my best fantasies is here in Crescent Ridge. The man who has called me a good girl, a dirty whore, and a cock slut.

I turn to face the man who feels less like a stranger and more like a lover. Tall with a broad frame, he has the kind of muscles you get from a gym rather than working outside. His dark hair is shorn short on the sides and longer strands are mussed on top. His beard is the same shade of brown, and neatly trimmed outlining his square jaw.

Above a large, pointed nose, his eyes are a warm melted caramel that freeze me in place. The rapid beat of my heart is loud in my ears, and I find myself struck silent by the tension pinging between us.

Eric

"Eric, say hello to Angie Miller," Liam says when I catch his attention.

I spotted him in front of the fire station surrounded by a bunch of other firefighters and thought it would be a good time to talk about the dining table I want to commission. I didn't see the petite blonde bombshell in skintight yoga pants and an oversized sweatshirt standing in front of him until she turned at the sound of my voice.

Her blue eyes are large glowing pools above a tiny button nose and pouty pink lips.

My mouth opens and nothing comes out. She watches me as I work my mouth in an effort to say the simplest greeting. Mortified that the most beautiful woman I've ever seen has watched me make a fool of myself I'm ready to turn on my heel and flee when her angelic voice stops me.

"Hello, Eric!" she says with a bright smile and a wave. "We were just talking about Poppy and William's success with the mail order bride program."

That's when I notice William standing off to the side with his arm around a brunette woman I've never seen before. The way she and William are absorbed in each other makes it obvious that she's his new bride, Poppy.

I nod at the happy couple, praying that Angie doesn't ask me a direct question.

"Eric and I signed up too," Liam says before I can panic about the searching look Angie's shooting my way.

"I can't believe a man like you would need to sign up for a mail order bride," Angie says locking eyes with me once again.

"Anything for love." I manage after a moment.

The resulting grin that stretches her cheeks and highlights her dimples makes the effort of speaking worth it.

"Eric does content creation," Liam says with a knowing smirk on his face.

He and William know about my job, including all the filthy details. Both have caught me in the middle of recording a time or two and love ribbing me about it. At one point Liam started calling me *Doctor Love*.

"Angie works from home as a project manager. We met at a yoga class in the park," Poppy replies before Angie or I can respond to Liam's comment.

"Eric is super into fitness," William chimes in before I can stammer my way through a compliment on Angie's career.

"I may have noticed," Angie whispers to me while our band of mutual friends continues to sing our praises.

I've tuned out the shameless nudging from our friend group as I look down into Angie's shining eyes. She's absolutely gorgeous and out of my league but I want nothing more than to whisk her away and never let her go.

Angie

"Your master plan went up in smoke," I tell Poppy once we're back at her and William's cabin.

"Did it though?" she replies with a sly smile. "I may have put my money on the wrong horse. True. But Eric caught your eye."

"All the men around here are eye catching," I retort while I take a seat on the couch.

In one hand I have a cold glass of lemonade, and in the other my cell phone which I'm scrolling through in an effort to find the mobile app for Pearl's Matchmaking. I stopped checking it after a while once I realized all the men trying to match with me were looking for a traditional wife to be a stay-at-home mom full-time.

That's just not what I want out of life.

A couple of kids would be nice. But I crave independence. The pride I feel knowing I can support myself and be successful is something I just can't give up. Ignoring my notifications I dive in. I'm a woman on a mission.

I spend an hour scrolling through profiles before I find Eric's.

If I hadn't met the man in person, I probably wouldn't have messaged him on the app. In fact, I almost missed his profile entirely while I was scrolling. He has one photo, and it's literally a picture of his profile in front of the mountain. The sun is setting behind the mountains and you can't see most of his face.

The bio section isn't to be found and he only included his hobbies. Working out and reading. I'm surprised he bothered to create a profile at all. He doesn't seem to be looking for a wife. But then I think about what he said about doing anything for love. Maybe like William he has trouble expressing himself. Poppy and William certainly had a rough start to their romance.

Before I overthink it, I send him a message asking him out to dinner. Poppy complains I'm being too direct as she reads over my shoulder.

"Flirt with him a little!" she says.

"You're too invested," I scold in return.

She takes a sip from her own glass of lemonade, wisely not addressing my reprimand. Poppy isn't trying to hide how badly she wants me to find my own mountain man here in Crescent Ridge. We've been friends for years and with her moving out here I've felt a little lost in Vegas. I don't leave the house as much and I spend too much time working without our lunches and yoga classes to distract me. It would be wonderful to find a husband and my own happiness out here.

But I'm only visiting for the long weekend, and I doubt I will manage to find a husband in three days. Even if my favorite content creator is a candidate.

I'm not going to get her hopes up. Not yet at least.

We sit down for dinner, and I leave my phone in the living room. I've checked it a dozen times and the radio silence on my date invite is becoming painful. I thought we had a moment at the fire station but maybe I was mistaken.

Maybe he's just not interested.

The longer my message goes unanswered the louder the silence becomes. The man said one word to me, and I've built up this epic fantasy of a romance in my brain. If Eric knew my thoughts he would get a restraining order.

Eric

I spend the rest of my day chatting Liam's ear off about Angie. Asking him questions about their conversation before I popped up. Seeking out every tidbit that William has given him over the past month.

At one point I start waxing poetic about how soft her hair looked while we're eating dinner and Liam finally snaps.

"Ask William for her number," he says while munching on a fry. "Ask her out or I swear I will push you into a ravine on our next hike."

Now that shuts me up. I may have found the woman meant to be mine but that doesn't matter if I can't talk to her. Liam must see the internal debate raging in my head because his frown softens.

"Text her," he says. "Tell her about the speech thing and ask her to dinner."

I step outside of *Lenny's* and call William before I can think twice about it.

"Hey, can you give me Angie's number?" I ask when the call connects.

"Oh, hell yes I can!" a woman's voice shouts into the phone.

She rattles off a series of numbers before I can process that Poppy answered her husband's phone. Something I honestly should've expected. William hates talking on the phone and Poppy is a chatty woman.

I add Angie to my contacts while Poppy carries on a one-sided conversation about how happy she is that I'm dating her friend. Even if I wanted, I couldn't get a word in, the woman talks a mile a minute.

By the time I faintly hear William calling his wife's name, she has told me a dozen things about Angie. From her favorite ice cream flavor to how much she likes pumpkin spice lattes and how much she likes her job.

"I gotta go, Eric. It was great talking to you. You're such a great listener!" Poppy says before disconnecting the call.

She didn't even let me say goodbye. Or remind her that I haven't asked Angie out and she hasn't said yes.

I shake my head with a smile on my face. If Angie talks half as much as her friend, my speech problem won't be an issue at all.

This is Eric. I asked Poppy for your number, and I hope that's okay.

I'm slipping my phone back into my pocket when it vibrates.

Hi, Eric. I'm so happy you got my number.

I stare at my phone grinning like a fool for a full minute before I reply.

Would you like to go on a date with me to the Fall Festival tomorrow? They serve pumpkin spice lattes at the coffee shop's tent and there is going to be a hayride down to the haunted corn maze.

A second later her response vibrates my phone again.

OMG yes! I'd love to!

I send her a follow up text and we agree to meet up in the parking lot of the park where the festival is being held at noon tomorrow. Her obvious enthusiasm leaves me feeling pumped as I return to my dinner with Liam.

"Thank you, sweet baby ranch. If I had to deal with you pining over that woman for one more minute I was going to run you over with my truck." Liam says while he finishes his fries.

"It wasn't *that* bad," I say with a wince.

His raised eyebrow says enough. We both know it was indeed that bad.

Angie

I wait by William's truck at the festival. Poppy and her husband wanted to wait with me, but I shooed them away. This isn't a friend hangout, it's a *date*. A first date at that.

Eric and I need to explore that spark I felt when we met, and I need to hear his voice again. Not to mention I need to tell him I recognize him from *Wicked Audio*. Before anything physical happens, he needs to know that much. And I have a feeling that we're going to get *very* physical *very* fast.

The banner for the festival hangs between two large wooden columns. It declares this the 22nd annual Crescent Ridge Fall Festival with two large jack-o'-lanterns on either side. Throughout the park I can see hay bales and rows of tents set up with the mingled sound of people talking and laughing as they walk through the festival.

My stomach begins to growl when I smell roasted corn and tacos. In addition to the food stalls, I see several food trucks set up along the path.

"Angie," Eric's deep voice curls around me from behind.

I spin to see him grinning down at me wearing a blue plaid flannel shirt and a snug pair of jeans. Suddenly I feel overdressed in a cream off shoulder sweater and black maxi skirt with my chunky heeled boots. The bat wing earrings might be a tad much.

But Eric doesn't seem to mind as he reaches out to hold my hand and guides me into the festival.

"I'm so happy you invited me on this date. I love spooky stuff!"

He listens as I ramble on about ghosts, ghouls, and goblins. By the time we line up in front of the local coffee stall I've rambled on about the paranormal for entirely too long.

"I'm so sorry," I say. "I'm steamrolling you. What sort of things are you interested in?"

He tenses beside me, his hand squeezing mine tightly as he does. The panicked look in his eye spurs me into another rambling monologue.

"You're probably the quiet type right?" I ask and he quickly nods. "Just pinch me when you want me to shut up."

His hand relaxes in my hold even though his frown doesn't melt away. I've never been with someone so painfully shy to the point they can't talk to me. And considering the filthy words I've listened to him say into a microphone his silence is odd. But we are in public so maybe he has an easier time talking one on one.

"Two pumpkin spice lattes, please," he orders when we reach the front of the line.

Before I can process that he knows my order he's whipped out his card to pay and we shuffle off to the side to wait for our drinks.

"Poppy?" I ask.

He dips his chin in agreement.

My friend is as chatty as I am. I know she gave him my number and I shouldn't be surprised that she gave him some pointers. I am a little miffed that he was able to talk to her without any problem.

He also ordered our coffee. And had no problem talking with Liam and William. Maybe he just has trouble talking to me.

As we grab our lattes and rejoin the crowd, I can't help but wonder why he has such a hard time talking to me. Waiting in line to get our faces painted I decide if this relationship is going to go anywhere, I need to rip off the band aid.

"I recognized your voice from *Wicked*," I confess just as he takes a sip of his coffee.

A second later he's choking on the hot liquid, coughing as I pat his back. My timing never fails. Bringing up a sensitive topic in public was a bad move. I shocked him into inhaling his drink rather than swallowing it.

"Next!" the lady running the booth calls out before we can talk about it.

I get a cute ghost painted on my cheek and after he refuses her idea of clown makeup, Eric gets a pumpkin.

Suddenly, not wanting to talk about the elephant I've invited onto our date I point at the truck pulling a trailer lined with haybales.

"Didn't you say there would be a hayride to the haunted corn maze?" I ask barely waiting for Eric to nod before I drag him off to join the next load of people riding down to the maze.

"I can't speak when you look at me," he says after we're seated.

There's a few other couples and a family with three children with us on the trailer but they're all wrapped up in their own conversations.

"Does that bother you?" I ask.

We should be talking about his work and if he's comfortable dating a fan. Especially one as obsessed with his voice as I am. He might not realize how often I've listened to his voice. That I've replayed his audios over and over until I could pick his voice out of a crowd. He has no idea how addicted I am, or he wouldn't still be on this date with me.

He shakes his head mutely and I remember that he can't talk with my eyes on him. I look away but he doesn't elaborate, and I begin to think he might be telling a white lie to spare my feelings.

A young woman with her blonde hair in a French braid joins our group at the last minute. She's carrying a picnic basket and wearing a bright blue sundress and white wedge heels. Her green eyes are sharp and vibrant as she sits next to me with a sweet smile.

"Hi Eric," she says with a little wave to my date.

"I'm Emma," she says to me without waiting for a response from Eric. "You must be Angie."

I nod but before I can say anything she's gushing about how nice it is that more women are moving to the ridge.

"I always lived in the city before I met Andrew. It's been quite the change going from the anonymity of city life to living in a small town where everyone knows everything about everyone. You should meet my husband before you go into the maze. It's time for his break so he won't be one of the one's scaring you," she says as we come to a stop next to a large field of corn.

The stalks are taller than Eric and we can hear the distant screams of people already in the maze. Solar lights low to the ground light the ground around the entrance and the path from what I can see is lit the same way.

"Andrew!" Emma calls out waving her arm in the air to attract the attention of a man dressed in black.

The only color is his white shirt that's rolled to the elbows underneath his vest. As he gets closer, I can see the white paint around his mouth looking like a wide smile and the black triangles around his eyes completing the look of a scary clown.

"Hey babe," he says when his blue eyes lock on her, completely ignoring everyone else around them.

She leans up on tiptoe to kiss him and once I realize it's more than a chaste peck, I have to look away in an attempt to give them privacy. Not that they're bothered by the public audience for their kiss.

Eric and I share a wry smile, and I laugh when he rolls his eyes at their blatant display of affection.

"Newlyweds?" I ask Emma when they come up for air.

"No, we've been married for two years," Emma says with a wide smile.

Her cheeks are tinted pink, and her eyes have a glazed look. Andrew's answering grin is almost as wide as his painted smile.

"Finally send off for your own bride, Eric?" he asks.

"No, she's visiting Poppy," he replies as Emma pulls me off to the side.

"Don't be too weirded out by the nosiness. It comes standard with the small town," she says with a knowing smile.

"It's different," I admit with a tight smile. "Were you a mail order bride?"

"No," Emma replies with a laugh. "Andrew and I met on SoulConnect. It was supposed to be casual sex, but we clicked right away."

I raise my eyebrows at her honesty, and she laughs.

"Trust me, it's hard to keep a secret around here. My friends visited soon after I moved in with Andrew and they teased me mercilessly about hooking up with a stranger in a remote mountain cabin. Word spread like wildfire after that."

Eric's secret isn't mine to tell so I tell Emma about meeting him on my first day in Crescent Ridge and how I felt a spark right away.

"It's our first date though," I add. "This thing between us could fizzle out."

Emma glances over to where Andrew and Eric are still talking. Eric's eyes meet mine and the heat I feel every time he looks at me burns through my veins.

"I don't think that's going to fizzle out," Emma says as she hands her phone to me, telling me to send myself a text so she'll have my number. "If you end up staying, let me know and we can get together sometime."

Eric and I watch as Andrew and Emma walk over to a set of picnic tables, their arms wrapped around each other.

"So, you like to listen to my voice when you come." Eric says looking off towards the corn maze. "You want to talk about that?"

Eric

My words are bold in the open air, but I can't take them back. They've been running through my head since she confessed to recognizing my voice. We might be in public but with everyone lining up for the maze and Emma and Andrew off at the picnic tables we're as close to being alone as can be right now. We're out of earshot and I can't wait another second to address it.

The thrill of knowing that she likes my voice, likes it enough to recognize it, has my cock pressing hard against the zipper of my jeans. The sheer amount of male pride is filling my chest to bursting.

"Here?" she asks in a whisper.

There are a few people milling about but most are in line for the roasted corn stall. I'm sure no one is paying us any mind, or I wouldn't have brought it up. Still the nervous tone in her voice is enough to have me pumping the brakes. I can wait.

"We can talk about it later," I say quickly.

I don't want her to feel comfortable.

"Over there," she says pointing at the tree line.

I follow her over to the pine trees watching as her shoulders relax the further away from the crowd we get.

"Emma warned me about the gossip grapevine," she explains once we're standing in a bed of pine needles.

"So, you like the sound of my voice?" I ask in a whisper.

Her blue eyes are on me, but I don't feel the words catching in my throat. The tightness in my chest is gone and as I watch her pupils dilate, I know her answer before she speaks.

"I love it," she says in a matching whisper.

My hands settle on her waist, the soft sweater bunching underneath my hands as her eyes pull me in, swirling like twin whirlpools.

"Tell me which one was your favorite," I say leaning down until our faces are an inch apart.

"Impossible."

Her warm breath blows out in a white cloud between us with the word.

"Liar," The word leaves my mouth before I can catch it.

It hangs between us and the smile that shows off her dimples soothes my anxiety over the brash accusation.

"I like when you tell me to earn it," she says to me. "When you growl low into my ear and tell me to suck your cock."

If we weren't in public, surrounded by neighbors and friends I would drag her into the woods. I'd have her on her knees, taking my cock into her hot little mouth and then her wet pussy in minutes.

"Are you going to be my good girl?" I whisper against her cheek. "Or are you going to be a dirty girl?"

Her cheeky smile stretches her red cheeks.

"Can't I be both?" she asks.

Rather than answer, I lean down to press my lips against hers. They're soft and supple beneath mine. She yields sweetly to me, opening to the press of my tongue and clinging to my shoulders as I hover over her.

Her nails bite into my shoulder through the thick flannel of my shirt reminding me that we're still in public. She whispers a muffled protest as I pull away, straightening to my full height.

"We should join the line," I say in a ragged whisper.

Angie shakes her head vehemently.

"Next time," she says tugging me towards the hay filed trailer for the ride back up to the festival.

Angie

Eric's square body truck has a leather bench seat in the front. After texting Poppy to let her know that I was going home with Eric, I slid to the middle. A moment later Eric climbed inside his truck and while his eyes widened, he didn't comment on my seat choice.

If I thought he disapproved of my choice those thoughts vanished when his hand landed on my thigh with a strong squeeze.

"Bold little thing, aren't you?" he asks after a moment.

His eyes are locked on the road in front of us as we wind our way up the mountain.

"One of us needs to be," I snark back without thought.

His booming laugh takes me by surprise as it fills the small cabin of his truck. We turn onto a dirt road as his thumb begins to rub the outside of my thigh in small circles of gentle pressure.

"It's becoming easier to talk to you," he says as he parks the truck in front of a large mountain cabin surrounded by pine trees.

"Why?" I ask throwing the loaded word between us without considering that it might set back our progress.

He looks at me directly, his caramel eyes dark with heat.

"I live in Crescent Ridge because I struggle to talk with strangers. As I warm to people, it becomes easier to talk to them. In a town where I can know everyone my speech doesn't have a large impact on my daily life," Eric says as he reaches across my body to unbuckle my seat belt.

A foolish part of me hoped he was tongue tied over my beauty. That he was so enamored that he couldn't find the right words.

"Normally it takes longer for me to warm up to people," he says as he helps me step down from his truck. "I didn't think I would be able to get two words out on our date. I was sure I'd be texting you halfway through just so you didn't find me weird and creepy."

I don't release his hand as we walk towards his cabin. His admission soothes my frazzled mind as his thumb strokes the back of my hand.

"It's not much," he says as he leads me into the cabin. "But it's home."

"Not much?" I ask twirling in a circle as we enter his living room. "It's fucking huge, Eric."

He chokes on a laugh as I look around the room. The soft blue sectional dominates the space in front of a large stone fireplace. The TV mounted on the wall is angled down and I can see a video game console sitting on the mantel beneath it.

The collection of soda cans and beer bottles on the coffee table marks this as a bachelor pad. The lack of décor adds another layer of confidence to the assumption. It's the middle of October and there isn't a pumpkin, or gourd to be found.

It's as I'm staring at his blank khaki painted walls that Eric wraps his arms around me from behind. A gentle tug has me leaning into his chest as his hands begin to explore my body.

"Let me know if I go too far," he whispers against the shell of my ear, his warm breath causing loose strands of hair to brush against my cheek.

He waits for me to nod before he gently pulls me towards a set of wooden stairs. More blank walls lead to a series of doors. We enter the last door and I nearly gasp as I step foot inside a gorgeous master bedroom. For all the lack of décor and personality downstairs this is very much Eric's space.

A large bed with an iron railing headboard takes center stage on a raised platform. The blankets covering it are a mix of creams and blues making it look like a sky full of clouds. He has dressers and a desk, each overflowing with knickknacks, and figurines. His bedside table is cluttered with mugs, one with his name printed inside a colorful outline of Colorado.

I take it all in as Eric steps behind me. His hands slip under my sweater to trace up my stomach until he is cupping my breasts through my bra. Even with the padded fabric limiting sensation I feel his fingers massaging them. I don't have to wait long before his hands are moving to find the clasp in the back.

"I want to take my time with you." His voice washes over me as he unhooks my bra.

My nipples harden as I slip my sweater over my head and let my blue lace bra slide down my arms. Spinning to face him I don't feel the burst of shyness I expected. With his eyes burning me with their hunger as he drinks me in, I don't feel anything other than bold.

"Do you taste as good as you look?" he asks me as he unbuttons his flannel shirt.

As he slips it off, my hands go to the firmly muscled chest it reveals. His tan skin is soft but the muscle beneath keeps it taunt. Eric lets me explore his chest, stroking my spine as my fingers trail down his stomach to his Adonis belt.

"You'll just have to find out," I reply as I unbutton his jeans.

He removes my hands and grabs me by the waist before he picks me up with ease and carries me across the room. My back hits the cloud of bedding just before he sinks to his knees at the edge of the bed.

"I bet you're delicious. My own personal little treat," he says as he unlaces my boots and tugs them off.

He flips up my skirt to press kisses along my thighs, each one higher and closer to my pussy than the next. But just when I think he's about to touch me properly he backs off. I grumble in protest, but he just chuckles as he helps me out of my skirt and panties.

"You're going to be completely naked for our first time, Angie," he says before settling his shoulders between my thighs.

He doesn't play or tease. His tongue licks a broad path through my slit, coating it in my arousal. Dipping his tongue inside me I let out a moan as he thrusts shallowly into my core. A moment later he withdraws, and I fight back disappointment at it being over so quickly. Before I can raise up to meet him for a kiss, his lips are attacking my clit.

He alternates sucking and nibbling as my back arches off the bed and I cry his name. I'm hanging on by a thread when he flicks the nub with the tip of his tongue.

I fall apart as he licks me through my orgasm. The sound of him moaning as he cleans my pussy as I come down will be one I always remember. The memory of his dark hair bobbing between my thighs with his eyes locked onto mine is one that can't be topped.

"Are you ready to take this cock, Angie?" he asks as he stands.

I watch with bated breath as he unzips his jeans. The black boxer briefs don't do much to hide the size of his cock or how hard he is as he looks at me sprawled across his bed. I must look a frightful sight. My hair is a tangled mess, and my body is limp from the aftermath of pleasure.

"Yes," I plead.

He crawls between my thighs, his length hanging heavy between us as he cages me in with his arms.

"Still, okay?" he asks.

"Yes," I reply. "I'm on the pill."

"Bare?" he asks with his eyes darkening into burnt amber.

I nod in response, expecting him to immediately push his cock inside me. He lowers himself until his cock is pressed against my pussy and he rocks his hips gently. Every slight thrust has the head of his cock bumping my over-sensitive clit pushing me right back to the edge of falling apart.

"Such a dirty girl, Angie," he whispers against my skin as he traces his tongue across my collarbone. "Letting someone like me take your pussy bare."

"I need it," I moan. "I need your cock, Eric."

His lips ghost over the pebbled nipple of one breast and I find myself grabbing his hair and wrenching his head back over it. The wiry hairs of his beard brushing the tender flesh as he moves. His lips curve into a salacious grin before he takes the hardened nub into his mouth.

Fire pours through my limbs as he flicks my nipple with his tongue. The rough texture of his tongue scratches at the sensitive flesh sending electric pulses through my body where I feel them echo in my core. More than ever, I need to feel him inside me.

My body clenches on nothing and the lack of anything filling me is driving me to frustration.

"Eric," I growl as he releases my nipple with a pop before blowing on it.

The warm breath hits my wet nipple like a chilly breeze. "Eric!" I shout.

His chuckle is evil as he switches sides, laving my other nipple with his attention as his hips continue to grind his cock against my clit.

"Please, baby," I plead as I arch my back seeking more contact. "I need to be fucked."

The feral gleam in his eyes breaks something inside me. Eric will keep teasing me until I can't take it anymore. If I want it, I'm going to have to take it. I wrap a leg around his waist and use the other to angle my body just right.

On his next thrust the head of his cock slips inside. I see Eric's eyes widen just before I wrap my other leg around him pulling my body towards his as each delicious inch of his cock sinks deeper into my pussy.

"Your pussy is so fucking needy," Eric says as he presses his hips down pining me to the bed in the process.

His mouth meets mine and I can taste myself on his lips and tongue as he kisses me. His teeth catch my bottom lip as he pulls away, biting down gently.

"Look at you," he says as he raises himself up. "Look how well your wet pussy takes my cock, Ange."

I watch as he pumps the hard length of his cock into me. It drags along my walls with each motion of his hips. I don't register the nickname at first, too overwhelmed by the sparks of pleasure building in my core as his thrusts pick up speed.

"Such a good girl," he rumbles. "Ange, my pretty little cockslut."

I claw at his back as he hammers into me, every brush of his pelvis against my clit sending me closer to the edge. The nickname makes my chest feel tight. More than the dirty words, the nickname feels personal. My name is already so short no one has ever bothered to call me anything else. But this man who wields words like a master calls me Ange.

I come all at once, pleasure bursting as I cry out his name as my body clenches. My pussy squeezes his cock, milking him as he fills me. His arms wrap around me cuddling me close as his hips stutter against mine until I feel his seed dripping from where we're joined.

When his head rises from my chest, and I see the questioning look in his warm caramel eyes I beat him to the punch.

"Still, good," I tell him.

I watch as a lazy smile spreads across his face as he gently lowers himself back down. His head is pillowed on my breast, the short strands of his hair tickling my chin and I've never felt so content.

Eventually I'll have to get up and go back to Poppy's, and then I'll have to go back to Vegas. I can already feel my heart breaking.

Eric

Waking up next to Angie and hearing her muffled snores is my new favorite thing in this world. The warm morning light caresses her skin as I relax in bed just looking at her.

The woman of my dreams is in my bed and already my mind is racing with plans for how to convince her to stay. She's not local and I know she lives in Vegas. Moving to the mountains isn't likely something she's considered but one of her friends does live here already. And she seemed to hit it off with Emma as well.

My thoughts turn to how easily I could pack up my life and move to her city. I work from home and aside from my selective mutism I could manage to live anywhere in the world.

I would have to leave my friends behind, but they would understand. William would move at the drop of a pin if Poppy wanted to live somewhere else. And sooner or later some woman is going to wrap Liam around her finger.

Angie's snoring stops abruptly when she wakes up. She stretches out her arms and legs out like a cat before shuffling closer to me.

"Did I oversleep?" she asks as she settles against my chest in a languid cuddle.

"It's Sunday," I say with a laugh. "You can sleep as late as you like."

She tenses before she sits up with a sense of urgency.

"Poppy and William expect me back for lunch," she says in explanation.

"It's early," I say rubbing her back. "The sun is barely up."

With an audible thump she slumps back onto the bed.

"Breakfast?" I ask.

"Please." Her words are muffled by the pillow and sleep.

"Don't move," I say with a laugh as I get out of bed.

I grab a pair of pajama pants from my dresser and lay out a second pair along with a shirt for Angie to wear when she wakes up again.

She emerges from my room an hour later as I put the finishing touches on breakfast. My shirt hangs down to her knees and the legs of the pants I gave her pool at her feet as she shuffles into the kitchen.

"I'm not a morning person," she says as she hugs me.

Her head rests heavily on my chest, her eyes still dazed with sleep.

"I record early in the mornings most of the time," I reply holding her close as I guide her to the table. "My sleepy voice is popular on *Wicked*."

I watch her for any signs of discomfort or jealousy, but she doesn't act bothered by my career. Something I feared when I thought about my future wife when I began working as an erotic audio content creator. Having her recognize me from my work avoids an awkward revelation, and her easy acceptance is a balm to my soul.

I can give up the mountain, but I've built a career and reputation in the space. It's all I know.

"Your slice of life audios are always so sweet," she says between bites of her waffle. "But I like hearing you talk in person so much more."

The tension in my chest eases and we eat our breakfast talking about anything that comes to mind. Angie tells me about the boba shop around the corner from her apartment and how she goes there every morning instead of the coffee shop. At least until pumpkin spice comes back on the menu every year.

"Favorite scary movie?" she asks at one point.

"Zombie Island." I reply and after a moment of thought she connects the dots.

"Scooby-Doo does not count!" she shouts between laughs.

"Those zombies were creepy!" I argue. "And that's about all I can handle in the horror category."

"I live for the terror," she says shaking her head. "You're gonna need to toughen up."

"Oh yeah?" I ask taking a sip of my water.

I watch her as she smirks over the rim of my glass. I might not like scary movies but if I get to cuddle up next to this woman on my couch, I think I will survive.

"Or you can hide underneath a blanket. Your choice."

"You're such a fucking brat, Ange," I growl.

"What are you going to do about it, Eric?" she replies with a smirk and an arch of her eyebrow.

"Remind you exactly who the boss is in our bed."

"I don't see a bed, do you?"

I pull her down onto my lap. The thin fabric of my pajama pants does nothing to mask my excitement. My cock brushes against her core as she rubs herself against me.

"Brats don't get fucked in bed," I whisper into her ear. "They get fucked on the kitchen table like a little slut."

"Oh, no," she replies with a roll of her eyes. "Anything but that."

"Be a good girl and grind that wet pussy on my cock."

Later after we've gone another round, and we're slumped across the kitchen table I send a silent thank you to the universe for sending me my perfect woman. The other half of my soul and the only woman to ever make me feel whole.

Angie

The sex was good. Better than good, it was fucking fantastic. Enough to make me want to extend my vacation indefinitely. It's not just the sex that makes me want to stay though. It's Eric, who is funny and kind. Who made me breakfast and treated me like I was something special.

But we both know our time together was temporary. How could it not be when I live hundreds of miles away? And we haven't talked about a relationship. We had a great time together but that's all it was. At least for Eric.

I can't help but feel that I'm leaving a piece of my heart behind with the mountain man.

So, when Eric drives me back to Poppy's, I'm thankful he doesn't try to make small talk. Doesn't try to let me down easily or try to stumble his way through a bumbling explanation about how long distance won't work.

He's quiet as we drive and that is perfect. Perfectly fine. Doesn't break my heart at all.

I knew from the beginning that this wasn't about forever. Eric may have signed up for that mail order bride website but he's not serious about settling down with someone. He either doesn't check his profile or he's ignoring my messages. I hate to think he could be so callous, but I haven't known him for long.

Now I'm going to spend one last afternoon with my friend and then I'm going to get on a plane and fly back home. And I'm never going to see Eric again.

Because I'm fuckable but not wife material.

As we park in William's driveway, Eric goes to open his door, but I stop him with a hand on his thigh. I unbuckle my seatbelt and lean over to kiss his cheek.

"Thanks for bringing me back," I say with a polite smile.

"Of course," He says, his voice sounding odd. Like he's enunciating the wrong syllables.

"We should do this again sometime," I say before hopping out of his cab and walking as calmly as I can manage to the cabin.

I don't hear Eric's truck leave until after I'm inside the house. The rumble of the motor fades away slowly as I let my smile slip away. I knew going into this it was a dead-end road. The only destination was heartbreak.

Eric

I don't know where I went wrong.

I just know that somewhere I missed a step. Angie was so detached when I dropped her off at William's cabin. Like we didn't just experience the same soul melding. She strides away from me on steady legs, her hips swaying as she enters the cabin without looking back at me once.

Numb, I drive back to my house on autopilot. I thought she would invite me inside or at least give me a chance to invite her on another date. To clear my head, I spend the afternoon in my home gym. I push every limit I have trying to erase her dismissive tone from my mind. If I could take a sponge and soap to my brain, I would.

As I'm toweling sweat off my face I hear the chime of an incoming text message. I trip over a dumbbell in my haste to check the sender. Disappointment sweeps over me when I see it's from William and not Angie.

Dumbass

Succinct and to the point.

I don't waste time texting him back. I need to know how I fucked up the best thing that's ever happened to me and he knows. I need to know now. He picks up on the third ring.

"Check your profile," he says in greeting.

I'm taken aback for a minute, before I remember the profile I created for Pearl's a while back. I did it mostly to appease the guys, not really expecting to find a woman who would want to move her entire life for a man like me. Not to mention just considering marriage to a stranger was unsettling.

"She messaged me?" I ask.

I don't know why she went through the trouble of finding me on the app when she has my phone number.

"Yep. And she's flying out today at four," William confirms before hanging up.

It takes a bit for me to remember my password for the app but once I'm logged in, I check my inbox. And there it is.

Dinner tonight?

The message is simple and direct, just like my Angie. And the time stamp is from the same day we met. She asked me out first and must have thought I ignored her.

Like a hammer striking my head reality hits me. She has a profile on a mail order bride matchmaking site. Clicking on her profile picture I read her bio and look through her photos. Unlike my profile she's filled hers out completely.

Looking for a mountain of a man who enjoys working out and wants to live life to the fullest. Bonus points if located near Crescent Ridge, Colorado.

I glance at the time on my phone noting that it's just past three. I don't have much time to catch her before she leaves. Grabbing a spare duffel bag, I stuff a few random clothes and my charger in it before snagging my wallet and keys off the kitchen table on my way out the door.

My truck makes good time to the airport and thanks to the small airport I'm able to buy a ticket last minute for her flight so I can get to her gate. People stare as I stride through the airport in my dirty workout clothes, but it doesn't bother me.

There was no time to change before I left, and I can't take any chances on missing my woman. I make my way through security and get to the gate where her plane is leaving just in time for boarding to start.

I see her from behind as she stands in line for boarding, her hair pulled back into a loose ponytail. The tight black yoga pants hugging her ass make my mouth water even as I pull out my phone and open the matchmaking app.

I cross my fingers that she has her notifications turned up as I hit send.

Angie

Waiting to board my plane I'm struck by how much I don't want to leave. Just thinking about returning to my apartment in the city with its sad little houseplants brings a frown to my face. My life seems so pale and boring now that I've spent the weekend in Crescent Ridge.

My phone dings with a notification when there are still a dozen people waiting to board the plane ahead of me. I bring it out prepared to switch it to airplane mode when I see it's a notification for Pearl's app.

I'm not ready to date another man. It might have only been one date, but I need time to move on from Eric. Still, the thought of ignoring the message doesn't sit well with me. I open the app planning to send a polite message and then switch my profile to private, but I'm brought to a halt when I see the notification.

It's not a message at all.

It's a marriage request, a digital confirmation that Pearl will use to track their success rate. And it's from Eric.

I look up from my phone with tears in my eyes. He's there, standing in front of me, holding a black duffel bag and a boarding pass. The orange tank top he's wearing is damp with sweat and his gym shorts are a garish green. Eyes wide and his sweaty hair sticking up in odd spots, he looks like he's ran the entire way to the gate.

"Ange," Eric says.

His voice sounds gruff and noticing that we're attracting attention I step out of line to let people move past me.

"You can't be serious," I say in disbelief.

It's not what I wanted to say. I want to say yes. I want to scream it from the rooftop. He doesn't appear fazed as he steps into my space. Towering above me he cups my chin in his hand to tilt my face up towards his. His caramel eyes swirl with urgency.

"Dead serious. I will marry you today. Hell, I was in love from the moment I met you. I don't care if everyone thinks I'm crazy for proposing after three days. I love you, Ange."

My breath comes out in a gasp as he leans down to kiss me. The wet warmth of my tears trickle down my face as he holds me close. His damp tank top is cold against my feverish skin.

"Yes," I say when we break apart. "I love you too."

The flight attendant that was checking boarding passes clears his throat and turning to look I see that the line of passengers has cleared and we're the only ones left.

"I packed a bag and bought a ticket," Eric says with a warm smile. "Just in case I couldn't convince you to come back home with me."

"All your recording equipment is here," I reply even as I shake my head at the attendant.

We're not going anywhere except straight back home.

"Let's wait a couple days before we tell them I'm staying," I tell him as we make our way back through the airport.

"Sounds like I get to keep you all to myself for a little while."

Eric's warm hand holds mine as we walk out into the warm sunshine. I take a deep breath of the crisp mountain air before I let him lead me across the parking lot to his truck.

There are a million details to work out. Moving cross country will be eventful for sure. But I know that Eric will be by my side the entire time. I came to Crescent Ridge just to visit my friend but now I've claimed my very own mountain man.

Epilogue

Angie

Six Months Later

"Look how pretty you are sucking my cock," Eric's voice growls into his microphone.

"Make me take it," I say breathlessly into my own microphone. "Use me like your little whore."

A month after I moved in with Eric, he floated the idea of doing a dual POV audio for his platform. I agreed, thinking it would just be a fun couple thing to try but the response has been overwhelmingly positive.

After a few months of recording with Eric I left my job as a project manager. Demand is high for dual audio and all the fans love it. We were even booked to record an audiobook.

As we pause the recording my husband looks over at me with hunger darkening his eyes.

"Oh, no you don't," I say as I stand up from my chair.

I slowly retreat to the studio door as he prowls towards me.

"We don't have time for sex," I say shaking my finger at him. "We promised Poppy we would be at her class's first recital, and I don't want to be late."

"They were late for our wedding," he says in response. "For the same reason."

I spin to race out of the room we use as a recording studio. I don't make it three steps into the living room before Eric's arms wrap around me. He sweeps me off my feet carrying me through the house straight towards our bedroom.

"Neanderthal," I scold swatting his brawny shoulder.

"Maybe we won't go at all," he says as he lays me down on the bed. "Maybe I'll just keep you busy in bed all day, like a true Neanderthal."

His lips find mine as we begin taking off our clothing. Eric's shirt peels off his body revealing an expanse of sinewy muscles that I never get tired of touching.

"Spread those juicy thighs and show me what's mine," he says.

My legs fall to the side at his command, my pussy already dripping as intense waves of heat pulse within my center. If I ever thought constant exposure to his voice would dull the effect it has on me, I've never been so happy to be so wrong.

"You make a man thirsty," Eric growls before settling between my thighs and hiking my thighs over his shoulders. "Let me clean the mess you've made."

Spread blatantly open for him the first touch of his tongue to my slit has me arching closer to his mouth.

"Eager little thing," he says laughing.

His laugh cuts off when I grab his hair and yank hard.

"Lick me like you mean it," I order, impatience turning my tone sharp.

Eric's tongue paints a trail of heat across my slit until he latches onto my clit. I see his eyebrow arch as his molten gaze meets mine and I know he's going to punish me for my tone.

Releasing my clit with a pop he returns to my entrance, thrusting his tongue inside me and curling the tip to torture me. I curl my fingers tighter into his hair, wrapping the soft strands against each digit until they turn white.

"Stop teasing," I murmur as he begins flicking my clit with the tip of his tongue.

Despite my protests that's exactly what the man continues to do. Just as I am on the cusp of orgasming, each time he switches things up. Over and over, he drags me to the edge only to pull me back at the last second.

When I'm a panting mess sprawled across the bed with my heart beating in time to the throbbing ache in my pussy, Eric finally crawls up the bed to cover my body with his own.

"How badly do you want it?" he growls low into my ear.

I glare at him in mute fury that only causes him to laugh. Reaching between us I grab his cock, choking him mid laugh. If he wants to tease and taunt, two can play that game.

I watch as he goes rigid above me, every muscle in his back and arms tensing as I stroke his length from root to tip.

"Ange." My name comes out in a pant as I rub my palm against the sensitive head of his cock in a circling motion.

"You want to tease me?" I purr. "Then you'll beg for the right to fuck me."

With each slide of my hand, he goes impossibly harder beneath my touch. A minute later I might as well be rubbing granite.

"Ange," he says through gritted teeth. "Please."

Another time I would flip us and continue the pleasurable torment, but I've already been pushed to the edge too much today. I release my grip on his cock as I hook a leg around his waist and pull him closer.

"Y-Yes," Eric says as he sinks his cock into me. "You're so wet my sweet little wife."

I drape my arms around his shoulders clinging to him as he begins rocking his hips. Our heated breath mingles between our bodies as every punch of his hips drives me closer to the edge.

"Give me everything. I want it all," I murmur as heat licks up my spine.

"I'm going to fill you up," he says pressing his forehead against mine. "Going to pump this pussy full of my seed. Breed you like the pretty little wife you are."

I fall apart, dark spots filling my vision, with his dirty words floating through my mind. He comes a second later with a strangled groan as his hot seed fills me.

We're late to Poppy's recital but judging by her knowing grin when we slide into our seats, I know she'll forgive us. After all she wanted me to find my own mountain man, she can't complain if my perfect man likes to keep me in bed.

I never thought I would find love in a small mountain town but life with Eric is filled with joy and love. As I sit in the theater curled against my husband, I can't imagine a better man to help me make a baby. Eric's large hand cradles my flat stomach as the ballet dancers prance across the stage.

Another few weeks and we'll tell Poppy and William about the baby. For right now it's just us and the happiness we've found in each other.

The End

Meet Jeb, the mountain man who prefers life in animal furs and living off the grid in Reclusive Mountain Man's Mail Order Bride.

You can sign up for my newsletter or follow me on Amazon to stay up to date on new releases.

Crescent Ridge Mail Order Brides

Crescent Ridge: Mountain Men In Uniform

A Bride For Thomas

A Bride For Scott

A Bride For Dennis

Crescent Ridge: Lumberjacks In Love

Sugar Maple
Apple Pine
Honey Oak

Pearl's Mail Order Brides

The First Mountain Man's Mail Order Bride

The Outlaw Mountain Man's Mail Order Bride

The Texan's Matchmaking Bride

The Texas Ranger's Mail Order Bride

Pearl's Modern Mail Order Brides

The Lighthouse Keeper's Mail Order Bride

Holiday Sweet Treats

Cinnamon Kissed

Sweetheart

Pumpkin Spiced Love

Monster Merge

Standalones

Dr. Ghoul's Girl
Ensorcelled
Spicy Shorts

Printed in Dunstable, United Kingdom